"He's young and foolish," she resolved.

"Yes! He's going to learn the hard way what it means to lose someone he loves. He'll regret it for the rest of his life."

"You sound like an authority on the matter."

"I am." He looked at her. "I lost you."

For a brief, uncomfortable moment, she was silent and he wished she would say something.

"I think we both sort of lost each other," she finally said.

His fingertips brushed against her face and he moved closer, waiting for her to stop him but she didn't. He wrapped his arms around her shoulders, pulled her into his chest. His nose gently touched hers, and then his lips kissed hers. She wrapped her arms around his waist, caressing his back. As the waves from the ocean crashed against the shore, his tongue danced against her mint-flavored mouth.

He still loved her. He knew it, and so did the universe.

Dear Reader,

This is definitely a story about second chances and falling in love all over again. Edward is strong and arrogant, and Savannah is his complete opposite. But together they make one another whole. She's always given in to Edward's plans and taken a backseat to his political endeavors. However, she's not giving in to Edward this time—it's her time to shine.

This time, she's doing what makes her happy for a change. She needs to travel to London to finally make things right with her mother—the woman who abandoned her as a child. And she doesn't expect anyone to understand, but if you grow up without a parent in your life, you understand that there's a void that needs to be filled.

Their breakup was hard, but there's no doubt the two are still in love. Anyone could see that, but it isn't until they make love on the beach in the Caribbean that the two figure it out. I hope you will enjoy Edward and Savannah's sweet love story. You'll also fall in love with Savannah's eccentric mom, Nyle—her shenanigans will keep you on your toes. Edward and Savannah's sweet little girl, Chloe, gives them all a reason to live and love. She's the glue that holds them all together.

Nyle blew it with Savannah once upon a time, but Chloe is her second chance, and she has no intentions of blowing it again.

I hope you continue to love the Talbots and make them your favorite family.

Visit my website at monica-richardson.com or email me at monica@monica-richardson.com.

Happy reading!

Monica Richardson

Second Chance Seduction

MONICA
RICHARDSON

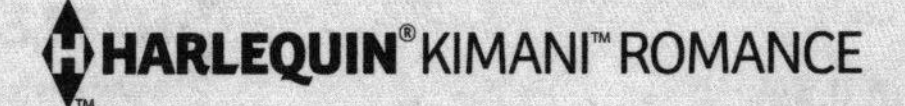

Recycling programs for this product may not exist in your area.

ISBN-13: 978-0-373-86459-1

Second Chance Seduction

For questions and comments about the quality of this book please contact us at CustomerService@Harlequin.com.

Printed in U.S.A.

Monica Richardson writes adult romances set in Florida and the Caribbean. Under the name Monica McKayhan, she wrote the Indigo Summer young adult series. *Indigo Summer* hit the *Essence* and *Black Issues Book Review* bestseller lists, and the series also received a film option. Monica's YA books have garnered accolades and industry recognition, including several American Library Association (ALA) placements on the Quick Picks for Reluctant Young Adult Readers and the Popular Paperbacks for Young Adults annual lists.

Books by Monica Richardson

Harlequin Kimani Romance

A Yuletide Affair
An Island Affair
Second Chance Seduction

Visit the Author Profile page at
Harlequin.com for more titles.

This is dedicated to my readers
who have fallen in love with the Talbot family.

Acknowledgments

To my readers who give me the energy
to continue to write great stories. I'm glad that you enjoy
the Talbot family. This is for you!

To my family in the Bahamas—visiting with you
and talking to you about my history has made the
research and writing of this Talbot series a complete joy,
especially Cameron and Raquel…you two have
really helped me to pull my research together!

Chapter 1

Edward stood across the room from her and admired long, lean legs, a round butt and perfectly exhibited breasts. Her hair was short and sassy, not long and flowing as when they were together. She smiled at the gentleman in front of her and then pushed her bangs out of her face. Edward was in awe of her for a moment. This wasn't the woman he remembered. No, this lady was self-assured and sexy—not the timid young woman that he once knew.

She finally looked his way and gave a nod of acknowledgment. It was her idea that they meet at her downtown office instead of her West Palm Beach home. He noticed that she was becoming increasingly uncomfortable with him visiting her space, even if it was for a good reason. The last few times, she'd suggested that they meet at a park or a restaurant to facilitate the exchange. Things had become much more impersonal, against his wishes.

She gave him a smile and headed his way. The smile, he remembered. It was genuine and wholesome—not to mention gorgeous. She led the way, and he followed her to a beautiful office with art that adorned the walls. The walls were painted in warm hues of orange—Savannah's favorite color. He immediately recognized the portrait of the colorful Eiffel Tower, an urban piece that they'd picked up when they honeymooned in Paris. He sat in the leather wingback chair and stared at the woman who sat across from him. He picked up the framed photograph from her desk—the one of their daughter, Chloe. *His girls*, as he used to call them.

"I talked to my mother the other day."

"Really?" He leaned back in the chair and glanced at Savannah's face. Tried to read her expression at the mention of her mother.

"Yes." Her face was blank.

It seemed that she was trying to shield her emotions from him, but he knew her all too well. He knew that her relationship with her mother had been strained and was the reason for many years of inner turmoil for Savannah.

"What was that conversation like?" he asked.

"It was long and—" a subtle little smile appeared in the corner of her mouth "—and genuine, actually."

"Really?" He was surprised.

"I'd like to go to London and spend some time with her."

"Okay, that's nice. A week or so?"

"Maybe longer."

"What about your job?"

Savannah exhaled and leaned her head against the back of the leather chair. "They're downsizing. Letting some people go. This is actually my last few weeks here."

"Savannah, I'm sorry." Edward crossed his leg over the other one. "What will you do? Have you been putting your résumé out there?"

"I'd like to look for a job while I'm in London."

"You're thinking of relocating there?"

She nodded a yes.

"What about Chloe?"

"She would go, too," she stated matter-of-factly. Like it was the most normal thing in the world to take a man's child clear across the world.

He took in a deep breath, gathering himself before he spoke again. But he could feel his anger boiling. His daughter meant the world to him, and he couldn't imagine her living in another state, let alone another country. He couldn't fathom the thought. Wouldn't. No. It was out of the question.

"You're not moving to London with Chloe." He was calm, but emphatic.

"Not right away, I know."

"Not at all!"

"You're being unreasonable, Edward."

He sat up in the chair. "How do you propose I see my daughter if you take her to England, Savannah? Are you going to fly her here for my weekend visits? And what about Christmas and summer breaks?"

He'd already found it difficult to manage a week without seeing Chloe's little face. He couldn't even imagine not seeing her for longer than that.

"We'll figure something out."

"We'll figure something out?" he asked. "She's just as much my daughter as she is yours, and I won't allow it."

"You're telling me what you won't allow? What gives you the right?"

"I have rights when it comes to my daughter. And I will exercise them if I need to."

"Are you threatening me?"

He stood. Headed toward the door. "It's not a threat, Savannah. It's a promise."

Their marriage had ended in divorce after a short eighteen months. It was the one thing that Edward had failed at. He'd excelled in college and breezed through law school. He'd run for mayor, and lost—but had landed a position on the West Palm Beach City Commission. A place where he could actually make a difference for the people in his community. However, the mayoral campaign had robbed him of his marriage. A newlywed with a pregnant wife at home, he'd gotten too caught up in his career. Not to mention he'd spent too much time with his beautiful campaign manager. Although he'd never cheated on Savannah with Quinn, the closeness of their relationship had caused more of a disturbance than his new marriage could take.

One of the best things about Edward's marriage to Savannah, though, had been their daughter, Chloe. He needed his daughter like the air he breathed. He needed to see her every single day. They'd become the best of friends. In her five years of life, he was astounded at the things that she knew. He didn't want to miss one single moment of her life. But now Savannah threatened to take it all away. He wouldn't allow her to do it. Couldn't.

"What do you want from me, Edward? Do you want me to put my life…my career on hold again?"

"This is not about your career, or mine for that matter. This is about our daughter. If you want to go to London to make amends with your mother and build a new career, that's fine. But don't take Chloe away from me. She's all I have."

"I couldn't leave her here. I won't," she said. "This is something I have to do, Edward. I'm sorry."

It seemed that he'd been dismissed.

"Get yourself a good lawyer, Savannah," he spat, and then stormed out of her office.

He needed air.

He walked briskly and managed to make it to the parking garage, loosened his tie and pulled a set of keys from his pocket. He collapsed into the driver's seat of his sedan and sat there for a moment. Listened while Omar Sosa's Afro-Cuban rhythms soothed his senses. He hated fighting with Savannah, but it seemed more frequent lately. Not long ago, they'd debated over which private school to send Chloe to and which curriculum would be better suited for her. They'd argued about whether to place her in a karate class or ballet. A week ago they'd argued about something as simple as Chloe's bob haircut. He thought she was too young for such a grown-up style. She was a kindergartner, for Christ's sake. He'd been active in every decision about his daughter, but not the one where Savannah planned to take her thousands of miles away. It seemed unfair.

He pulled out onto Clematis Street and breezed through the yellow light. His heart ached. He scrolled through the address book on his phone and looked for Jack Wesley's phone number. He didn't want to involve his attorney—in fact he'd only said it to get Savannah's attention—but he needed to know what his rights were regarding his daughter.

"JW!" Edward exclaimed. "How the hell are you?"

"I'm making it," Jack said. "Trying my best to keep a good law practice and maintain a happy marriage all at the same time."

"Well, I can't help you in that area, bro. I failed tremendously at my marriage."

"You failed because you didn't put in the effort. Savannah was a good woman."

"All of that is neither here nor there."

"Do you miss her?" Jack asked.

"What? Of course not," Edward lied. He would never let his friend know that he regretted every moment since Savannah left. "She has her life and I have mine."

"Right," a skeptical Jack said.

"I didn't call you to talk about my failed marriage to Savannah. I need some advice regarding Chloe."

"What about Chloe?"

"Savannah's trying to take her to London…to live! Can you believe that?" Edward asked. "I need to know what my rights are."

"Have you had lunch already?"

"Not yet."

"Meet me at the little chicken and waffles spot on Okeechobee in thirty minutes."

"Bro, fried chicken and waffles? How about something a little healthier?"

"You're still on that kick," Jack stated. He sighed. "Have you completely given up meat?"

"No, of course not. I've traded red meat and pork for chicken, fish and tofu. I'm just eating healthier, man, that's all."

"I see. You choose, then."

"Darbster. Dixie Highway."

"Do they have anything that resembles meat?"

"Tofu." Edward laughed.

"Ah, man."

"Keep an open mind," said Edward. "I'll meet you there in thirty minutes."

Edward hit the end button on his phone. Turned up the volume on his music. He was anxious to speak with Jack. Surely he would receive some good advice from his old friend. Jack would tell him exactly how to go about keeping his daughter in the country. He felt better already, less helpless. Cocky, even.

He slid into the booth at the restaurant and gave the menu a quick scan. He already knew what he wanted—it was a place that he frequented often. He ordered his usual meal and then ordered something for Jack.

"And bring two glasses of water, please," he said to the female server.

He raised his hand when he saw Jack walk through the door. His friend looked worn, as though he needed a vacation. He removed his suit jacket and slid into the booth across from Edward. Gave him a strong slap of the hands and a handshake.

"Good to see you."

"Likewise." Edward grinned. "I took the liberty of ordering for you."

"And why would you do that?"

"Because I know this isn't your kind of place," Edward said, "but you'll be thanking me later."

"You think so?"

"I know so."

Soon the server arrived with two piping-hot plates of food and set them down in front of the men. Jack frowned at the sight of his.

"Don't knock it until you try it," said Edward.

"I'll try to keep an open mind."

"Good," Edward said, and then went on to explain what transpired at Savannah's office earlier.

"You overreacted, bro." Jack frowned as he picked over his meal. He pushed the tofu aside and managed to get the vegetables into his mouth. "But you do have rights regarding your daughter. The question is, are you up for a fight with Savannah?"

"I can't let her take Chloe away without a fight."

"Perhaps you two can work something out without involving the courts. Summer is approaching. Maybe you can convince her to let Chloe spend the summer with you. You'd deliver her to London safe and sound in the fall, just before school starts. Maybe you can get her again around Christmastime or spring break."

"That won't work," Edward said emphatically. "I need to see her at least once a week. And besides, we have a custody plan that says I get her every week. She can't just wake up one morning and decide she wants to move to the other side of the earth."

"Well, if you're not in agreement with the move, then Savannah must file a petition for relocation with the court. The family court judge will take into consideration what's in the best interest of the child. Stuff like how Chloe's relationship with you will be impacted if she takes her away. Also, how the move will impact her mental, physical and emotional development."

"Okay."

"And whether or not the relationship with you can be preserved…kind of like the arrangement that I suggested in the beginning."

"Can't be preserved," Edward said.

"Then once she files, we have a short deadline to object to the move," Jack said. "I'll get the paperwork started as soon as I return to my office so we'll be ready."

"You're a lifesaver, man." Edward smiled. Exhaled.

"We'll have to contend with a court hearing. Maybe even a trial, if it goes that far." Jack sipped on his ice water. "Are you up for that?"

"What choice do I have?" Edward said. "I'm up for it if she is. She started this whole thing."

"I'm just asking, because I know it's been a long, hard road for you and Savannah in the past. I was just wondering if you're willing to go down that road again."

"I don't want to fight with Savannah again. It was a painful time."

"I remember. I was right there with you."

"Yes, you were. You've been a great friend."

"I just hate to see you go through that again. And you two have finally gotten this co-parenting thing down."

"Right. We have."

"You've made it through some tough times. Not to mention that whole bogus engagement thing Savannah had with her corny boss." Jack grinned. "If you can make it through that, you can make it through anything."

"Don't remind me of that fool."

Jack laughed. "You were so jealous."

"I wasn't jealous!"

"You were beyond jealous. I knew then that you were still in love with that woman."

"What?" Edward denied Jack's claims. "I'm not in love with her. I do love her *in a family sort of way*...kind of like I love my sisters."

"Yeah, I don't think you love Savannah like you love your sisters." Jack laughed. "But if that's your story..."

"That's my story." Edward laughed, too. "And I'm sticking with it."

"Maybe you should just move to London, too," Jack said.

"Go to hell!" said Edward.

"I'm only kidding, bro. I know this is a serious situation for you." Jack wiped his mouth with a cloth napkin. "Let me see what we can work out. Perhaps we won't have to go to court at all."

"That would be great."

Savannah had surprised him with the divorce. She'd claimed that she needed to get away and had gone to Georgia for a lengthy visit with her father. After several long weeks, instead of returning to their home in Florida as Edward had anticipated, Savannah had decided to stay in Georgia with her father. Soon she'd had Edward served and completely caught him off guard. And if divorcing him wasn't enough, she asked for alimony and child support. She wanted the family home and asked that he continue to pay the mortgage until she was gainfully employed. He wouldn't be blind-sided by her again.

In fact, when he was done reading Savannah her rights, she wouldn't know what hit her.

Chapter 2

Savannah was young when she married Edward. Her pregnancy had been difficult, and Edward had insisted that she stay home with Chloe for her first two years.

"I'll take care of us," he'd said.

"What about my career? My goals?" she'd argued. "I have dreams, too."

"Give me time. When I'm mayor, you can go back to work."

It was too much for Savannah. She'd become invisible to him. He'd stopped coming home at a decent hour. She was alone more times than not, and she'd become lonely. She'd even suspected that Edward and his campaign manager, Quinn, were more than friends. She'd cried too many tears. Begged Edward for a reprieve.

"I can't focus when you're on my back all the time," he'd complained.

Finally, her father convinced her to come to Georgia for a visit. "You and the baby," he'd said. "That way you can figure things out."

Savannah, Georgia, had been her home for most of her

life. She was named after the city with cobblestone streets and Spanish moss hanging from ancient trees. Her father, a decorated officer in the military, had retired there—it was his home. He'd met Savannah's mother while stationed in Germany. Nyle Carrington had taken the train from London to Germany for a weekend getaway with girlfriends, and returned to her home in London engaged to a US soldier. They dated for a short time, and soon, Frank Carrington's wife-to-be was pregnant with their new bundle of joy. When Savannah was two, her father's tour of duty was over, and the couple moved to his home in Georgia. Nyle found life difficult in the States, and soon returned to London, leaving Frank behind to raise their toddler alone. She sent cards and gifts for birthdays and Christmas, and occasionally she returned for short visits. Each visit, she'd promise to stay. She'd fill Savannah's head with stories of her home in London and promises that the next time she came, she'd take Savannah back to London with her. Instead, Savannah would awaken the next morning or return from school, only to find her mother gone again. By the time Savannah reached puberty, she'd given up any hope of having a normal relationship with her mother. She'd resolved that Nyle would never be a part of her life. And once she was an adult, she'd cut off all communication with her.

Until now.

Nyle was aging and needed Savannah in her life. She was remorseful and admitted that she hadn't been the best mother. She wanted to meet her only grandchild and realized the importance of having Savannah and Chloe in her life now. Savannah by all rights could've turned her back on the woman who'd abandoned her, but the truth was, she needed Nyle, too. Her life had been incomplete for so long, and she was ready to be a whole person. She wanted Chloe to know her grandmother and to learn about the history and her family in London. She needed to give their relationship a chance.

Conversations with her mother had become more frequent. They talked every day the way mothers and daughters were supposed to. They experienced moments that Savannah had only dreamed of in the past. They talked about Savannah and Chloe coming for a long visit—maybe even permanently. With Savannah's company downsizing, it seemed like the opportune time.

Nyle invited her to share her flat until she found her own place. Savannah would leave Chloe in Florida with Edward until the school year ended. She'd go there and get settled before coming back for her daughter. She was an experienced designer and already had an interview lined up with a prominent company. Her plans seemed perfect, flawless. And the anticipation of reuniting with her mother was all that mattered now. It was important to her, and she couldn't see why Edward didn't understand. He knew the history of her relationship with Nyle. They'd had plenty of conversations about it. She'd cried on his shoulder more times than she cared to remember, and he'd comforted her, given her encouragement. Loved her all the more. She expected him to be the one person who understood this burning desire. But instead, he was the one giving her grief.

"Have you had lunch?" Jarrod walked into her office as he often did, without knocking, and plopped his medium frame down in the chair opposite her desk. He studied her with those light brown eyes and gave her that bright smile that she loved so much. He was nicely built with dark curly hair and a strong physique that he worked for at the gym too many times a week, in her opinion. He was always sharply dressed.

"No time," she said.

"You have to eat," said Jarrod. "Why don't we go grab a bite?"

"I can't. I have a ton of work to finish up here."

"I'm giving you permission to take a lunch break." Jarrod laughed. "I'm the boss. And frankly, you're a workaholic."

"I have a meeting with a buyer this afternoon, and I want to be prepared."

"I appreciate your commitment to this company, Savannah. Even in the wake of my selling it."

"I love my job."

"And you're damn good at it." He smiled. "Which reminds me. I just got off the phone with an old colleague of mine, Herman Mason. His company specializes in women's fashion. One of the largest in England. I got you an interview."

"Are you kidding? Herman Mason?"

"I told him you were my best fashion designer, and he's very interested in meeting with you when you arrive in London," he said.

"Jarrod! I don't know what to say."

"Say that you won't embarrass me. Show him what you got." He smiled. "It's the least I can do, considering I can't keep you around here."

"I appreciate it. More than you know."

Jarrod became more comfortable in his seat. "I heard the commotion that went on…earlier…with your ex. Is everything okay?"

"Everything's fine."

"You need me to rough him up a little bit? Teach him a lesson?" Jarrod grinned at his own joke.

Savannah laughed inside. She knew that Jarrod could never stand up to Edward. Not physically. Not otherwise. The two were very different. When she met Jarrod, she wanted something so different from Edward that she'd gone to the other extreme. Jarrod was doting, gave her all the attention she wanted and needed—and sometimes more than she wanted. He wasn't afraid to share his feelings. Edward was a man's man. He would never admit to anything, and was hardly ever available to her. The two were like night and day. Both were gentlemen and loving, but Edward would rough Jarrod up if given half a chance.

"That won't be necessary. Edward's harmless."

"I know you still have a thing…for him…"

"Don't start, Jarrod. Please."

"It's why we didn't work out, isn't it?"

"We didn't work out because we just weren't meant to be." Savannah kept the conversation light. She knew that the tone had the potential to change—fast. "I appreciate everything you've done for me. You're a great friend."

Jarrod stood, headed toward the door. A slight smile danced in the corner of his mouth. "So I've been placed back into the friend bucket."

Savannah laughed. "Yes."

"Anything for you and Chloe."

Jarrod disappeared before Savannah could say another word. She did appreciate him, in spite of the fact that their whirlwind fling hadn't lasted. He was the first man she'd dated after the divorce. He'd romanced her and given her all the attention that a woman desired from a man—the attention that she'd desired from Edward. He'd even fallen in love with Chloe, and would've made a wonderful stepfather. When he'd asked Savannah for her hand in marriage, it seemed the only logical next step—except for the fact that she didn't love him. She thought he was a nice catch, a successful man any woman would be happy to have. But she didn't feel for him the things that he felt for her. He didn't care if she didn't love him—he wanted her anyway. She would grow to love him, he'd told her.

"Love is overrated anyway," he'd insisted. "People put too much emphasis on it. Successful marriages aren't built on love, they're built on commitment."

That way of thinking didn't sit well with Savannah. She needed love, and she wouldn't settle for anything less. He was devastated when she broke off the engagement, but it didn't stop him from trying to change her mind every chance he got.

Jarrod knew fashion inside and out. He'd been in the business a long time and had taught Savannah much of what she knew. His company had taken the industry by storm. But suddenly it was on a downward slope. Sales had fallen and the business was suffering. He needed to downsize, and as much as he wanted to retain Savannah, he couldn't afford to keep her. Soon Jarrod's Fashions would be owned by someone else.

Savannah shut the door to her office to avoid any other interruptions. She took a seat at her drafting table, her sketches scattered about. She thought of Edward. Wanted to call and smooth things over with him. Her decision to go to London hadn't been meant to hurt him. She wanted him to understand her need to connect with her mother. They'd come a long way since the divorce. They'd become more than just co-parents—they were friends. And she didn't want to jeopardize their friendship. But it was her time. He'd always come first in their marriage—his career, his feelings, his everything. It was the thing that had torn them apart. She'd taken a backseat for long enough. Now it was her time to do the things that made her happy.

She'd already anticipated that Edward might not be amenable to her idea of relocating with Chloe. Her income wasn't as adequate as Edward's and she didn't have attorney friends to assist her. She'd already done her research and learned that there were forms that needed to be filed whether

Edward agreed or disagreed with the move. So she'd already downloaded the necessary forms for both scenarios. She'd hoped that they could come to an agreement and that the decision would be consensual. However, Edward had been all but tolerable. The news was sudden, and he needed time to absorb it. Soon, he would see that he'd overreacted. But if not, she would take him to court.

Chapter 3

Edward sat sunk back in the leather seat of his car and watched as youngsters hopped into their parents' vehicles. The petals of a plumeria flower rested against the leather seat, right next to a plastic bag filled with Laffy Taffy, Nerds, Milk Duds and Skittles. He watched for Chloe. Expected her to rush to his car as she had every single Friday afternoon—her thick ponytails would be flying in different directions, the plaid skirt that she wore would be twisted in the back, and she'd offer him the biggest snaggletoothed smile that he loved so much.

Surely she remembered it was Friday. And not just any Friday, but the one on which her favorite movie came out at the theaters. They would smuggle the bag of candy into the auditorium in her backpack. They would order a large bucket of popcorn and a large Coke to share, and they would sit in the middle of the theater. Not too close to the screen, but not too far in the back. Right in the center.

Miss Jennings marched out of the school, a row of kindergartners following close behind. Edward sat straight up in his seat. He didn't want to be caught slouching as he scanned the row of children in search of his daughter. When he saw her, he smiled. Her ponytails flew in opposite directions, just as he'd suspected. She rushed to the car when she spotted him, Miss Jennings following close behind. Chloe pulled on the door handle and hopped inside. Miss Jennings stuck her head inside.

"Hello, Mr. Talbot." She gave him that same flirty smile that she always gave him.

The first time he saw the smile, he thought he was mistaken. Thought it was innocent until the time she gave him a raise of the eyebrows followed by a slip of her phone number during a parent-teacher conference. He never called. Feared that it would be a conflict of interest, dating his daughter's teacher. Not to mention, she wasn't his type.

He'd dated a few women after the divorce. Freda was the attractive psychologist that he'd met at a conference. She was the total package—beautiful, smart, independent. A nice catch, but she was too bossy. She wanted to dress him and mold him into what she wanted him to be, and he wasn't that type of man. He had his own agenda. Miranda was conservative and laid-back, accommodating. Too accommodating for his taste. She was the total package, too—beautiful, smart, independent—but there was no mystery. He'd managed to find something wrong with every woman he dated.

"Hello, Miss Jennings." Edward was cordial.

"Her homework is in her backpack," she said.

"Thanks."

"Have a great weekend, Chloe. I'll see you on Monday."

"Bye, Miss Jennings!" Chloe exclaimed before shutting her door. "Hi, Daddy!"

"Hello, Princess." He tapped the side of his face until she leaned over and kissed it.

"How was school?"

"Awesome!"

"For you, madam." He handed her the single yellow flower.

She smelled it and then stuck it into her hair. "It's pretty, Daddy. Thank you."

"You're welcome."

"You got the goods." She grinned wickedly as she peeked into the plastic bag filled with candy. She fastened her seat belt.

He knew that he shouldn't let her ride in the front seat. She was supposed to be buckled up in her car seat in the back, but some days he made an exception. And this was one of them.

"I got the goods." Edward smiled as he pulled out of the school's parking lot.

Chloe stuffed the bag of candy into her backpack. "What time does the movie start?"

"Four o'clock," he said. "If we hurry, we can make it before the previews are over."

"Cool." She toyed with his stereo until she found her favorite satellite radio station. She sang along with Katy Perry.

The theater was crowded. It seemed that every child in America had shown up for the premiere of the movie. Edward purchased tickets and then the two made a beeline for the concession stand. He held on to Chloe's hand.

"How's your mommy doing?" he asked as they stood in line.

"She's fine," said Chloe. "She misses you."

"Really? How do you know?"

"She talks about you all the time."

"Really," he asked, and tried to seem unfazed by her remarks. But he couldn't help prying. "Like what?"

"I don't know, Daddy. Just saying stuff like 'your daddy and I used to listen to this type of music' or 'your daddy really likes this kind of food.'"

"I see," said Edward.

"Do you still love her?"

"I will always love your mom. And you. We're always going to be family."

"Even when we move to London?"

"Your mom talked to you about London?"

"She said we're going to live with her mother, Nyle."

"How do you feel about that?"

"I don't want to go, Daddy. Please don't make me go. If we go there, I won't get to spend the weekends with you anymore."

"Don't worry, baby. You're not going anywhere." Edward kissed Chloe's hand. "I'll make sure of it."

He intended to speak with Savannah about filling his daughter's head with her fantasies of moving away. As soon as the movie was over he'd confront her.

At home, Edward poured himself a glass of Merlot and began to prepare a vegetarian Caribbean meal for two. Being reared in the Bahamas, he'd learned his way around a kitchen. Growing up in a large family with three sisters and a mother who could cook, he was spoiled. Never had to worry about cooking. But after marrying Savannah, he was forced to become a great cook, considering his wife could barely boil water. He would call home to his mother in the Bahamas and she'd equip him with her recipes.

After his father's heart attack scare, Edward had become obsessed with his diet—only feasting on fish and chicken and incorporating more vegetables into his diet. He insisted on healthy eating in order to prevent heart disease and other ailments that bad eating caused. He needed to be healthy for his daughter, and he wouldn't compromise that. He visited the gym every other morning, if for nothing more than a run on the treadmill.

"You think you can break up the broccoli?" Edward asked Chloe.

"I can do it." She stood on a step stool in front of the kitchen's island with the granite top.

"Good!" He pulled her ponytail. "You do the broccoli and I'll cut up the peppers and onions."

He headed into the living room and tuned the stereo to his Afro-Cuban playlist. He could hear his phone ringing in the kitchen.

"Daddy, it's Mommy!" Chloe called from the kitchen.

He grabbed it from the granite countertop and answered it. "Hello."

"Hi." Savannah's voice was sweet in Edward's ear. "What's Chloe doing?"

"She's preparing vegetables for our dinner," Edward said. "We're making a vegetarian gumbo."

"Yum. You always were a great cook," said Savannah. "The movie was great, I hope."

"It was fantastic," Edward said. "Your daughter fell asleep midway through, but I enjoyed it."

Chloe laughed, and so did Savannah.

"She's so bad at movies."

"The worst." Edward laughed. "Would you like to speak with her?"

"I actually called to speak with you. I'd like to talk to you about London."

"There's nothing more to talk about." Edward was calm for Chloe's sake.

"I would really like your blessing, Edward. I would hope that we could come to an agreement about it."

"That won't happen," he said, and then smiled at Chloe,

who was listening intently. Edward stepped outside onto the back deck where he could speak freely. "I haven't changed my position on this, Savannah."

"Would you really deny me the opportunity to connect with my mother? You of all people know how important this is for me."

"Then *you* should go to London and connect with your mother. But leave Chloe."

"I can't leave my child, Edward. You know I would never leave her."

"Then you won't be going. Because she's not going!" He was adamant. "I would never agree to that."

Savannah was quiet for a moment. "Then I don't have a choice. I'll have to petition the courts. I don't want to, Edward, but you're leaving me no choice."

"Do what you have to do, Savannah. But know that I will fight this."

"I know that you already have your bulldogs lined up," she said, referring to Edward's lawyer friends.

"I've already consulted with counsel. Yes."

"Fine."

"And just so you know, Chloe doesn't want to move to London. Have you considered that?"

"You've been talking to her about it?"

"She brought it up," he said. "Apparently you've been filling her head with this bullshit."

"How dare you discuss this with her without me."

"You've created this, Savannah! So deal with it."

"I will!" she yelled and hung up.

Edward stood on the deck for a moment, trying to gather himself before going back inside. If Savannah was looking for a fight, she'd surely found one.

After dinner, he tucked Chloe into her bed.

"Are you mad at Mommy?"

"No, sweetheart. I'm not mad at your mommy," he lied. The truth was, he was furious with his ex-wife. "Now get some sleep. You're in charge of the pancakes in the morning."

"Me?"

"Yes, you."

"Good night, Daddy."

"Good night, baby." He kissed her forehead.

He poured himself another glass of Merlot and plopped down on his leather sofa. Turned on CNN to find out the latest goings-on in the world. He leaned his head against the tan leather and thought of Chloe. He didn't know what he would do if a judge found that she'd be better off in another country. He wouldn't survive without her, and thinking about it took his breath away. He blocked it from his mind. Thought about work instead, and before long his eyes grew heavy. He gave in to the fatigue.

When he pulled up in front of Savannah's home on Sunday afternoon, his emotions got the best of him. Usually, she'd suggested that the drop-off take place somewhere else, but this time she wanted him to drop Chloe at home. In the past, when he'd dropped Chloe off there after his weekend, he would at least walk her to the door. Occasionally, Savannah would invite him inside for a cup of coffee and a quick chat. But today he wasn't in the mood to stand on her doorstep, and even less in the mood for a conversation with her. He sat in the driver's seat of the car, leaned over and kissed his daughter.

"I love you, sweetheart," he said.

"Love you, too, Daddy. You're not coming in?"

"No, not today, baby. I'll wait here until you go inside."

Chloe hopped out of the sedan and skipped to the front door of the two-story traditional brick home. The home that he and Savannah had shared before the divorce. The one that he still made mortgage payments on. She rang the doorbell and within seconds Savannah appeared in the doorway. She took Chloe's backpack and gave her a strong hug. She glanced toward the car, as if waiting for Edward to step out of the car or at least wave. He refused to do either of the two, and as a result she ignored him, too. She grabbed Chloe's hand and went inside, shutting the door behind her.

He sat there for a moment. Part of him hoped she'd return and at least beg him to come inside, start a fight or something. He needed to engage with her, even if it was negatively. With a long sigh, he slowly pulled away from the curb. They'd reached an impasse. And the only logical move was to allow the courts to make a decision. They'd been down this road before, allowing the system to decide the fate of their family. They had vowed never to do that again, to allow a third party to come into their lives and make decisions for them. They were educated and reasonable, and fully capable of deciding what was best for Chloe. However, they had broken yet another promise. They had all but started a war.

Chapter 4

Savannah sat in the third row of the auditorium, a wide grin on her face as Chloe glided across the stage, dancing on her toes to "Für Elise." She'd been practicing the routine for months, forcing Savannah to watch as she stumbled over her own feet too many times. But tonight she was graceful and poised, and she beamed with pride. Savannah lifted her phone into the air as she recorded the event. The seat next to her was empty. She'd saved it for Edward in the event that he made it on time. She hadn't spoken with him in days. It was obvious that he was still bitter about their last encounter.

She looked around the auditorium and then took a quick glance at the door. She searched for him and finally spotted him standing at the back of the auditorium, his tall frame leaning against the wall. She always thought that Edward was a handsome man with a wonderfully built physique, light brown skin, a nicely trimmed goatee and a Bahamian accent that drove women wild. His tie was loosened a bit, and he looked exhausted. It appeared that he'd made it there in the knick of time, just moments before Chloe's performance. Their eyes connected and she smiled, gave a subtle wave. He nodded a hello. She pointed at the empty seat next to her, but he kept his eyes focused on the stage—pretended not to see the gesture. Edward could be stubborn. And so could she.

After the recital, she searched for him again, but he was nowhere in sight. She couldn't believe that he would leave without saying goodbye to Chloe, or at least letting her know that he'd been there. A light breeze brushed across the palm trees as she and Chloe stepped out into the night air. Edward stood near the door, waiting for them outside. Savannah exhaled. She was glad he was still there. When Chloe spotted him, she rushed over to him.

"Daddy!"

He lifted her into his arms and kissed her cheek. "Hey, sweetheart."

"Did you see? I didn't make any mistakes."

"You did good."

"Hello, Edward." Savannah gave him another warm smile.

"Savannah." He was cold.

They walked toward Savannah's car as Chloe filled his ears with everything that had gone on over the course of her day.

"Sweetie, why don't you sit in the car and wait for Mommy? Let me have a word with Daddy," Savannah said.

"Okay."

Savannah unlocked the door, got inside, started the engine and turned on the air-conditioning. Chloe hopped into the backseat and snapped the seat belt around her booster seat. Savannah got out and shut the door behind her.

"About the other day—" she began.

"Don't even worry about it. It's okay," he interrupted.

"Edward, I don't know how to fix this."

"What are your plans, Savannah? Are you moving to London or aren't you?"

"I am."

"Then what is there to fix?"

"I'm not trying to hurt you. I'm just trying to do something for me for a change."

"Without regard for your daughter…or me," Edward argued. "Doesn't it concern you at all that she'll be so far away from her father? You women are all the same. You want a man to step up to the plate and be a good father, but then you won't let him."

"Don't try to make this about all women or send me on a guilt trip."

"If you're feeling guilty, then maybe it's your own conscience." He walked toward the rear of her car and beckoned for Chloe to let her window down. "Good night, sweetheart. I'll see you this weekend."

"Good night, Daddy."

He walked past Savannah and headed for his car. "Good night, Savannah. Drive safe."

She stood there. She'd been dismissed, and she didn't like it one bit.

She drove home, her heart beating fast. Edward had a way of getting under her skin. She glanced into the backseat, gave Chloe a warm smile. Didn't want her daughter to notice that she was uneasy or angry. She bought Chloe a Happy Meal from McDonald's and headed home.

When she stepped into the house, it felt stuffy from the Florida heat. She walked across the shiny hardwood into the kitchen and opened a window to let in some fresh air. She loved the home. She and Edward had it built to their own specifications. The hardwood had to be raisin-colored, and the ceilings had to be yea high. Edward had been very specific about the dimensions of the backyard and the square footage of his man cave. Almost immediately after the divorce, his man cave had been transformed into her home office. She'd painted the walls a soft pink as a tribute to her heartache.

Chloe rushed upstairs to her room and Savannah pulled the last load of laundry from the dryer.

"Chloe!" Savannah called. "Chloe, come and get your sneakers off the stairs, please."

The phone rang as she made it halfway upstairs. She headed back downstairs to the kitchen to grab her phone. "Chloe! Your shoes."

"Mommy, can I have an ice cream, too?" Chloe stood in the doorway of the kitchen.

"Give me a minute," she said and picked up the telephone receiver. "Hello."

"Savannah," the caller whimpered on the other end.

"Nyle?" Savannah dropped the basket of clothes onto the tile floor. "What's wrong?"

"They put me out."

"Who?"

"My landlord. Put me right out onto the street. I have nowhere to go."

"What? Why would they do that?"

"I don't know, Savannah. Times have been hard. I missed a couple of payments. All I know is that all of my stuff is out on the street, and I have nowhere to go."

"What about Aunt Frances? Why don't you go there?"

"We don't get along very well. I've burnt my bridges with her. She won't let me stay."

"Maybe I can talk to her."

"I don't know, Savannah," said Nyle. "When are you moving here?"

"I'm working on it." Savannah sighed. "I need some time to wrap things up here."

"I'll be homeless by the time you get here."

"Maybe you can just come here for a while. I'll send you a ticket." Savannah thought that was a perfect idea. It would resolve her problems with Edward, and at the same time give Nyle a place to go.

"I can't. I have to live in London. It's my home," Nyle said. "It's why your father and I…our marriage didn't survive. He wanted me to live in the US."

"He wanted you to live in the US because it's where he was…where your child was."

"I know you blame me for leaving you, sweetheart. But he wouldn't allow me to take you."

Nyle's story suddenly sounded eerily familiar. Edward was giving her the same resistance that her father had given Nyle. Only Nyle was willing to leave without her daughter. Savannah wouldn't make that sacrifice. She wouldn't leave without Chloe. Of that, she was certain. She would fight him.

"I can send you money to help you get into a place. It's the best I can do."

"I just need a deposit and first month. After that, I can make it on my own. And I promise to pay you back as soon as you get here. I promise."

"I'll wire you some funds in the morning," Savannah said. "Do you have somewhere to go until then?"

"I'll see if my neighbor will let me crash on her couch for the night."

"Good. I'll talk to you tomorrow, Nyle."

"Kiss Chloe for me," she said.

"I will."

"I can't wait to meet her," Nyle said. "I'll talk to you tomorrow."

She was gone, just as she had always been during Savannah's life. She felt the emptiness and yearned for her mother's presence. Leaving Florida would tear her and Edward apart, but she needed to be in London—to right the wrongs of her past. She needed it like the air she breathed.

Chloe stood in front of her, sneakers in hand. She grabbed her daughter's face in her hands and kissed her forehead.

"Are you okay, Mommy?"

"I'm fine, baby."

She was all but fine.

Chapter 5

Edward leaned back in his chair as he was winding down his call. He spun around and gazed out the window at the view of the marina from his office. He quickly jotted down a few notes and then looked up. Quinn was standing in his doorway. He held his finger up to her and she gave him a smile. He admired her curves in the dress she wore. She was a beautiful woman with a five-foot frame, dark flawless skin, braids and the deepest of dimples.

Quinn had been his biggest fan, the cheerleader who supported his every venture.

He finished his call and then hung up.

"What's up?" he asked.

"We're all headed over to Bailey's for a drink. It's Martin's birthday. The big four-o. Can you believe he's that old?"

"Doesn't look a day over thirty-nine," Edward teased.

"You're coming, right?"

"I'm gonna pass. I have a lot to finish up here," said Edward. "And not really in a celebratory mood."

"Really? Why?"

"Just not feeling up to it today."

"You want to talk about it?"

"Not really. No."

"If you don't want to talk about it, then you have to at least come have a drink. It would be rude not to." Quinn smiled. "Come on, dude. I'm not taking no for an answer. Leave your car and I'll drive."

Edward contemplated her offer. The truth was, he needed to unwind. The entire work week had been trying. He was grateful for Friday, although his Monday morning hadn't gone well at all. He hated fighting with Savannah. He felt as if he needed to protect her, yet he was always hurting her. He was stuck in a hard place. He wanted her to be happy, but not at the cost of losing his daughter. She was all he had. Sure, he'd graduated from one of the most prestigious law schools in the country, Harvard. He'd been at the top of his class. He had practiced law at one of the top law firms and had almost won the mayor's office. He had a gratifying career as a council member and soon he'd make a decision to run for the senate. And although he'd failed at being a husband to Savannah, with fatherhood he'd been given a second chance to make things right. He wouldn't gamble with that.

"Fine. Give me like twenty minutes to wrap things up," he said.

"I'll meet you in the lobby in thirty."

Quinn had loved Edward from the moment they'd started working on his mayoral campaign. And he knew it. She had placed her own career on hold to support his. A paralegal in the prosecutor's office, she'd always been ambitious. It didn't surprise him one bit when she landed a job in the mayor's office. He knew that she loved him, but he never acted on it. He also knew that he would never love her the way she wanted him to. Not the way he loved Savannah. He would never commit to her. Not even sexually. He felt that a sexual relationship with Quinn, even after his divorce from Savannah, would violate everything he loved and honored. His reluctance only made her try harder, and having Edward in her life and her bed had always been her one ambition. But he kept things at arm's length. He enjoyed her friendship and never gave her any reason to think there would be anything more. In fact he'd always told her that he loved their friendship just the way it was; didn't want to tarnish it. He'd always made it clear that he wasn't interested in her that way, and he respected her too much to give her false hope.

His six-foot-two frame sank into the passenger's seat of her Mercedes coupe. He moved his seat all the way back and reclined. "Please drive the speed limit today," he warned.

"Excuse me. I always drive the speed limit." Quinn smiled and adjusted the volume on her music.

"And no rap today..."

Before he could finish his sentence, Nicki Minaj's vocals permeated the car. Obscenities drifted into the air as Quinn let the convertible top down and pulled out of the parking garage.

"Buckle up," she said and then zoomed down Okeechobee Boulevard.

When they stepped into the bar, their colleagues had already snagged a table near the window. John Palmer raised his glass into the air to get their attention. The birthday boy was on the dance floor with a tall, sexy woman. Dollar bills were pinned to his shirt. Quinn took a seat at the table and Edward made his way to the bar, where he ordered a round of drinks for his colleagues. At the table he began to feel the music and bob his head.

"We should dance." Quinn leaned in and tried to speak over the music.

"If it isn't Edward Talbot," Martin interrupted.

"Happy birthday." Edward gave him a strong handshake, ignoring Quinn's offer. "What are you, like fifty now?"

"Minus ten, bro," said Martin. "And I'm sensitive about it, so no jokes."

"You should be glad to see another year," Edward said. "What are you drinking?"

"Vodka tonic. And not the cheap stuff. I want top-shelf." Martin laughed.

"You got it."

"I'm glad you came out to celebrate with me. I feel pretty honored," Martin said. "Take a walk with me to the bar."

Edward excused himself and followed Martin to the bar. "What's up?"

"The election year is fast approaching. What are you doing about the Florida Senate race? Are you running or what?"

"I'm still undecided."

"You should run. You can win this," said Martin. "You should've won mayor. No doubt you were the most viable candidate."

"I appreciate that, but I'm happy in my current position."

"Should you decide to run, I'm willing to invest in your campaign. I'm there for you, like you were for me when I ran for city commissioner."

The mayoral campaign had cost Edward his marriage. He'd been gun-shy about running for any office higher than the one he held as city commissioner. His current position as city commissioner required less of his time and allowed him to spend more quality time with Chloe. He liked it that way.

"I appreciate the support," said Edward, "and should I decide to run, you'll be one of the first to know."

Edward's phone vibrated in his pocket and he pulled it out, looked at the display. Savannah was calling. He was happy to see her smiling face on the screen of his phone, because she certainly hadn't been smiling when he saw her in person. She'd had a change of heart, he hoped. Perhaps she was feeling a bit of sorrow—much as he was feeling about their last interaction. A reprieve was exactly what they needed.

"Excuse me, Martin. I need to take this," he said and then walked as far away from the music as he could get. He answered the phone. "Hello."

"Edward?" the sweet voice on the other end asked.

He could barely hear and decided to step outside the bar. He stood on the patio. "Hello. Savannah?"

"Edward, I'm at St. Mary's with Chloe."

"Oh my God! What happened?"

"Her asthma again. She was running a pretty high fever when I picked her up from school. She's been complaining of chest pains. So I brought her to the emergency room."

"Has she seen the doctor?"

"Not yet. We're waiting."

"I'm on my way," Edward said before hanging up.

Unfortunately, Chloe had battled with asthma for most of her life. It usually flared up in the spring when pollen was high in Florida. She suffered so much and so often that it broke his heart. And every incident and flare-up became more serious than the one before, and it devastated him that he couldn't fix it. He was her father, her protector, and he couldn't protect her from her illness.

As soon as he hung up the phone, it dawned on him that he hadn't driven. He found Quinn and appealed to her to drive him back to his car.

"The hospital is closer," Quinn said. "I'll just take you there."

Edward wanted to protest. The last thing he wanted to do was show up at St. Mary's with a woman Savannah had accused him of seeing for years. But Quinn had been correct. The hospital was a closer drive, and he needed to get to Chloe as quickly as possible. He hopped into the passenger seat of Quinn's convertible and she drove him to the hospital. She pulled into an empty space in the parking lot.

"Do you need for me to wait for you? Or come inside?"

"No. I'll be fine."

"You want me to come back and pick you up?"

"No, I'll manage. It will probably be late. I'll just grab a taxi."

"You sure?"

"Absolutely. I'll be fine." He opened the car door. "Thanks a lot for driving me."

"Call me if you need me," she said.

Edward walked into the emergency waiting room. When he didn't see Savannah and Chloe, he inquired at the front desk and was informed that she'd just gone back to see the doctor. He was allowed to join them. Savannah looked frantic and defeated, but her eyes lit up when she saw Edward. He went straight for Chloe and kissed her forehead.

"Hi, Daddy," she weakly said.

"What's going on with my favorite girl?" he asked.

He'd always called Savannah his favorite girl, too. He hoped the comment would get under her skin.

"I don't feel good," Chloe whined.

Savannah cleared her throat. "The doctor thinks it might be asthmatic bronchitis. They're going to do a test called Spirometry test, which will measure her lung function."

He nodded and acknowledged her statement, but didn't really look her in the eyes; he was too embarrassed about their last conversation and still a bit angry. He took note of how beautiful she looked in her two-piece blue business suit, but tried to keep his attention focused on his daughter.

Hours passed before they received the results of Chloe's Spirometry test that confirmed that she indeed had asthmatic bronchitis. The doctor handed Savannah a prescription and gave Edward a strong handshake. They were given instructions on how to care for Chloe and then sent on their way. It was late, and Edward felt exhausted as they took the silver elevator down to the first floor.

"Where'd you park?" Savannah asked.

"I actually left my car at the office. I caught a ride over from the bar with a coworker. We were celebrating Martin's birthday," said Edward. "I'll just grab a taxi."

"Do you need a ride?" Savannah asked.

"Would you mind?"

"No. Not at all." She pulled her keys from her purse. Held them in her hand. "I'm right out front."

"I don't want to take you out of your way, so you can just drop me off at home. I'll take a taxi into the office in the morning," Edward said. "Besides, you need to get this one home as soon as possible. Get her to bed."

"We have to fill her prescriptions first."

Edward climbed into the passenger seat of Savannah's practical four-door sedan. It was one that she'd purchased after their breakup. He'd offered her the family SUV after they'd parted, but Savannah had complained that she wanted something a little more economical.

"That Lincoln Navigator, although very nice, is a gas guzzler. I want something that gets good gas mileage—a nice little Toyota or something." She was the levelheaded one and way more practical than Edward. She'd kept him grounded. It was what he loved about her.

They'd traded the Navigator for a fully loaded Toyota. She toyed with the buttons on the stereo until she found something mellow. She seemed nervous. She and Edward had become friends and co-parents for Chloe over the years, but it had been a long time since they shared such a small space together. He tried to lighten the mood by commenting on her music.

"What is it we're listening to?' he asked, and then switched to a hip-hop station.

"Who listens to that?"

"Normal people." He smiled and then looked out the window.

They stopped by the drugstore, and soon Savannah pulled up in front of Edward's home. Waited for him to step out of the car.

"Daddy, I'm hungry. Can you make me your special soup?" Chloe asked before her father exited the car. "It'll make me feel much better."

Edward gave Savannah a knowing grin. "It's really late, baby. Mommy can grab you some soup on the way home."

"Please, Daddy," Chloe sang. "I want *your* soup."

"What do you think?" Edward asked Savannah.

"I don't know." Savannah was hesitant.

"Please, Mommy," said Chloe.

"She's pretty convincing," Savannah stated, and put the car in Park. "I guess it'll be okay. Your soup is pretty easy to make."

"I have all of the ingredients here," Edward said. "I just need you to cut up the papaya for me. If you don't mind."

She'd always helped Edward prepare his papaya soup—a Bahamian recipe that he'd prepared on many occasions. It was Chloe's favorite, and Savannah's, too.

"Okay, Chloe." Savannah sighed. "But then we're going home and getting you medicated and in bed."

Edward stepped out of the car first and opened the back door for Chloe to hop out. He picked her up and she wrapped her legs around him. He carried her to the front door. Savannah locked up the car and followed. Something inside Edward felt joy that they were staying. Maybe he would have an opportunity to talk to Savannah about London again, and this time he'd convince her to stay or at least consider leaving Chloe with him.

Chapter 6

Savannah chopped the papaya while Edward sautéed onions and melted butter in a saucepan. Caribbean music drifted through the air. She could count on one hand the number of times she'd entered Edward's home, and never past the living room. She'd picked Chloe up from there a few times and was always careful not to invade his space. In particular, she didn't want to run across a loose earring or a pair of women's panties. She usually stayed in her place.

"Care for a glass of wine?" Edward asked Savannah.

"Sure."

He turned the fire down low and then opened a bottle of Riesling. Poured two glasses and handed one to Savannah. After cutting the papaya, she took a seat at the kitchen's island and sipped on wine. She watched as Edward combined the ingredients of his soup together. As it simmered, he took a seat across from her.

"Aside from Chloe's trip to the ER, how was your day?" he asked.

"It was going pretty smoothly," she said. "It changed everything when I found out that my baby was sick."

"I know what you mean. My heart sank when I got your phone call."

"I knew you'd want to know that she was sick."

"Thank you for calling me."

"I'll always let you know what's going on with her. You're her father, and I know that you love her."

"I love her very much."

"How was *your* day?" Savannah changed the subject before Edward brought up the move.

"It was a pretty good end to the work week."

"So it's Martin's birthday." Savannah smiled. "I like Martin. He's a good man."

"He is a good man," said Edward. "He offered to help with my campaign should I decide to run for the senate."

"Are you considering it?"

"Somewhat."

"That's good." Savannah took a long sip of her wine. "Why the hesitation?"

"Chloe, of course," he said matter-of-factly. "I'm aware that a campaign might take up too much of my time, and I want to make sure she's my priority."

Savannah wanted to say that with Chloe moving to London, he'd have more time on his hands to pursue his political ambitions, but she avoided any conversation about London. The mood was very casual and friendly. She didn't want to bring up anything that would start an argument. Instead of responding, she just nodded.

"I'm not keeping you from anything, am I?" he asked. "Did you have plans tonight?"

"Yeah, Chloe and I had plans to watch *Sofia the First* for the umpteenth time. Then I planned on watching her fall asleep and I'd be watching it by myself." Savannah laughed.

"Yeah, I've seen *Sofia the First* more times than I'm

willing to admit. And I also won't admit that I actually liked it." Edward laughed and then went to the stove, stirred his soup. "I think it's ready."

Edward pulled three ceramic bowls from the shelf. Ladled soup into each one. He placed a bowl in front of Savannah. "Taste."

Savannah took the spoon and scooped a spoonful into her mouth. Closed her eyes. "Mmm. Just as I remember."

Edward grabbed a spoon, put it into her bowl as if it were a perfectly normal thing to do and tasted the soup. "Not bad."

"I'll go get Chloe." Savannah put down her spoon. She hopped down from the bar-height island stool and went into the den.

Chloe lounged on the sofa and was sound asleep. She considered waking her, but decided against it. Her daughter seemed too peaceful. She walked back into the kitchen where Edward was already enjoying a bowl of papaya soup.

"She's asleep, huh?"

"Yes. And I didn't want to wake her."

"Let her sleep," he said. "Sit down and enjoy your soup."

Savannah did as Edward suggested. The two of them ate soup and enjoyed light conversation. When they were done, they cleaned the kitchen together.

"It's late. We should probably get going," Savannah said.

"Yes, it is late, and I don't like the idea of you two driving around West Palm Beach at this hour. Why don't I tuck Chloe into her bed, and the two of you just spend the night? Go home in the morning." Edward suggested.

Savannah wanted to protest. Not because she didn't want to stay, but she needed Edward to know that she wasn't the passive young girl that he remembered from before. She had changed. She was a strong woman now, with a mind of her own, and she wouldn't give in to his every whim.

"No, we're going to go." She stood her ground.

"Do you really want to load Chloe into the car and then unload her when you get home?" he asked. "She's asleep, and not to mention she's sick."

He had a point.

Savannah exhaled. "I suppose it would be easier to stay here, get a good night's sleep."

"I have fresh bedding and could prepare the guest room for you."

Initially, Savannah thought the evening would be awkward, considering she and Edward were in the middle of a battle. Not to mention, she'd just filed a petition to take Chloe out of the country. The papers would arrive at his office on Monday. She contemplated the drive home and decided that spending the night would be a wiser choice.

"Fine," she said.

Edward carried Chloe to her bedroom, and Savannah followed. She found pajamas in the chest of drawers and undressed Chloe, while Edward disappeared down the hall to prepare the guest room for her. She tucked her daughter beneath the covers, kissed her. Edward stepped back into the room, pulled the covers up to Chloe's chin.

"Good night, sweetheart," he said.

"Good night, Daddy."

"You missed the soup," he told her.

"I'm sorry, Daddy, but I was really sleepy," she said.

"Well, get some sleep, and we'll have breakfast in the morning."

"Are you spending the night, too, Mommy?"

"Yes." Savannah gave her daughter a warm smile. "I'll be in the room right down the hall if you need me. Okay?"

"In Daddy's room?"

Savannah glanced over at Edward, who had a light smile in the corner of his mouth. "No, baby, in the guest room."

"Okay," said Chloe. "Good night, Mommy."

"Good night, baby. I'll see you tomorrow." Savannah stood, kissed Chloe and followed Edward to the door.

Edward turned off the light and pulled the door, leaving it cracked a little.

"You can sleep in Daddy's room if you want," Edward teased.

"No thanks," Savannah said, and playfully rolled her eyes.

"Your bed is ready, then…whenever you're ready for it," he said. "Can I get you a T-shirt or something to sleep in?"

"Sure. That would be nice."

Edward disappeared into his bedroom and returned with his favorite Harvard T-shirt.

"Thanks. I remember this shirt. It's a little faded," she teased.

"It's gotten a lot of use," he smiled. "You should feel honored that I let you wear it."

"I do. Nobody's ever been allowed to touch this shirt. I wasn't even allowed to wash it with the other laundry back in the day." She giggled, took the shirt and headed toward the guest bathroom to put it on.

"That's right! And you should handle it with care," he said.

"I will." She gave him a wink before popping into bathroom.

In the small powder room, she took a curious peek into the medicine cabinet. She wasn't sure what she was looking for, but felt the need to be nosy. Wondered if she'd find an extra toothbrush or evidence that someone had been there for any length of time and left something behind. It was exactly what she'd avoided before, but suddenly her curiosity got the best of her. The cabinet was virtually empty, with the exception of a small bottle of Tylenol. She grabbed a washcloth from the linen closet and washed her face, then stared at her reflection in the mirror for a moment. Her day had been long, and her evening with Chloe at the emergency room had been trying. Spending the night at Edward's place wasn't the norm, but the thought of driving home after her rough day had been an exhausting thought. She was grateful for his offer, but wouldn't get too comfortable. She just needed to get through the night, and then she'd be on her way in the morning.

She walked past Edward's master bedroom. The light was on and the door was ajar. She took a quick peek as she crept past. His room was immaculate with a masculine-looking comforter on the king-size bed. She remembered that Edward had always been a neat person. It was one of the things that they shared in common. She never had to clean up behind him. His California king bed was neatly made, and everything seemed to be in its rightful place.

She wanted to catch the news before retreating to the guest room for the night, so she made her way into the den area. Edward, wearing a pair of pajama bottoms and a crisp white T-shirt, lounged at one end of the sofa, the remote control in his hand.

"Oh, I'm sorry. I didn't know you were still up. I wanted to catch the news before I turned in. If you don't mind," Savannah explained.

"I don't mind at all. I always watch the news myself before bed," said Edward. "I still have trouble sleeping."

"Still?" She plopped down at the opposite end of the sofa.

"I'm up way past midnight every night and then up at the crack of dawn every morning. I usually get less than six hours."

"That's not very healthy. Particularly for a man who is more health-conscious than anyone I know."

"It's not healthy, but it's my reality." Edward stood. "I'm going to have another glass of wine. You care for one?"

"Sure," she said.

He disappeared into the kitchen and then returned with an open bottle of wine and two glasses. He handed her a glass and poured wine into it. She curled her feet beneath her bottom, made herself at home.

"What a trying day," she exclaimed as she took a sip of wine, then leaned her head back and sighed.

"Chloe gave us quite a scare with that high fever."

"I was pretty scared when I received the phone call from her school. She's my baby."

"Mine, too," he reminded her. "After the divorce…you know…well, she's all I have."

"I know how you feel about your daughter, Edward." She wanted to clear the air, address the elephant in the room. "And I'm not trying to hurt you by taking her away. I'm just trying to do something for me—something to make me happy for a change."

"I get that, Savannah," he said. "I don't like it, but I get it."

"I've put my life…my dreams on hold for so long. It's my time."

"I get it. It was all about me…always. My career destroyed our marriage, robbed us of our family. If I could go back and change it, I would."

Savannah was shocked by his words. She'd never heard Edward admit that he was wrong—let alone that he would change his actions if given a chance. After she'd filed for divorce, he had begged her to stay, but she'd always been convinced that he only begged because he thought it was something that a man should do. That she had bruised his ego. That a breakup would blemish his political ambitions.

"What would you have done differently?" She was really curious.

"It wasn't a good time for me to run for mayor, I admit. Not as a newlywed with a pregnant wife. I would have waited until our marriage was more mature, able to handle the campaign."

"I could've been more understanding," she admitted. "You were certainly young and ambitious. I was just so damn insecure."

"You were beautiful. *Are* beautiful. What would you have to be insecure about?"

"For starters, I weighed a ton when I was pregnant." She giggled.

"You were beautiful when you were pregnant."

She blushed at his comment, but said, "Your campaign manager was slim and beautiful, and very much into you."

"Quinn?"

"Yes, Quinn." She said, "Don't act like you're surprised."

"She was my friend. Still is."

"And in love with you! Don't forget that part," said Savannah. "She had more access than me. And I was jealous of her. She had more of you than I did."

"She was the last person you needed to worry about."

"But I did. I worried."

There was an awkward moment of silence.

Edward looked her square in the eyes. "I'm sorry."

"It's okay. Water under the bridge." She stood, finished her wine and placed the glass on the coffee table. "Now we have Chloe, and she's our focus."

"And we have to do what's in her best interest. Whatever that is."

"And we will."

"If you leave with Chloe, my life will be empty," he said. "And not just because Chloe's gone. But you. Truth is, I'll miss you, too, Savannah."

Tears almost welled in her eyes. She headed out of the room before he saw her vulnerability. She needed to be strong. "Good night, Edward."

He sighed. He was losing her already, just when he'd gotten her to open up. "Good night."

Savannah made her way to the guest bedroom. She shut the door securely behind her and stood with her back against it. For the first time in years, those old feelings had returned—myriad emotions of love, anger, jealousy and fear. She felt confused. She had long moved on since their breakup, but couldn't understand what she was feeling at that moment. She had used her father's home in Savannah, Georgia, as her refuge—a place to heal and get over Edward—and she thought she had.

After graduating from art school in Georgia, she'd landed a job in Florida, and decided that it was time to move back to Florida and face Edward again. Her daughter needed a father and she wanted to make their co-parenting work. She had even found romance again—with a man who promised her the world. Though he wasn't Edward, whom she was still madly in love with, she accepted his proposal of marriage. She wanted a better life for Chloe and for herself. And even though it hadn't worked out with him, she was sure that she had recovered from Edward. Until now.

She walked over to the bed, pulled the covers back. She shut off the light and climbed into bed. She just needed to get through the night. Tomorrow she and Chloe would go back to their normal life—the place where she could rid herself of whatever it was she'd just felt after her conversation with Edward. She closed her eyes tightly and prayed for sweet dreams, not the ones that used to haunt her so many nights before.

Chapter 7

Edward flipped the wheat pancake and browned the other side. He checked on the turkey bacon that sizzled in the oven. He warmed maple syrup in the microwave and cut up fresh honeydew melon and pineapple into chunks. The kitchen table was set for three. He was determined to surprise Savannah and Chloe with breakfast. He hoped that he could make up for upsetting her. She'd obviously been bothered by their conversation the previous night. He'd made so many mistakes with her. He knew that he had gotten it all wrong before, but he wanted to make things right. And hopefully, in the process, he could convince her to stay in Florida.

The part of Savannah's heritage that was white and black Caribbean was the part that had always connected with Edward. Her mother was a white Londoner and her father's ancestors had hailed from the Dominican Republic. Their Caribbean roots had transcended all. From the moment Edward saw her, he knew he would make her his wife. He wanted her. He loved her. But he was young—and life had become overwhelming. Though his father,

Paul John Talbot, had been the perfect role model, Edward had completely ignored his teachings. The signs were all there—that his marriage was ending—but he didn't see them. Not until Savannah had completely relocated to Georgia with their infant daughter. And even then, he thought she was being unreasonable and was confident that she would return home soon. It wasn't until he was served with an order for divorce that the reality hit like a ton of bricks. His marriage was over.

He should've fought harder, made more sacrifices, but he was cocky—blamed her for everything. She should've been more understanding of his career, of his need to succeed. Didn't she know that everything he did was for their family? Yet it hadn't been enough. In his mind, she'd been the selfish one, ungrateful even. He had regretted every moment since then. Everything he thought she'd been, time had proven him wrong.

"Good morning." Savannah was completely dressed in the business suit she'd worn the day before. The strap of her purse securely on her shoulder and keys in hand, she stepped into the kitchen. "Chloe's getting dressed. We're headed home."

"But I cooked breakfast. At least stay and eat."

Savannah looked around at all that he'd prepared and seemed to contemplate his offer.

"Please. Be a shame to waste all of this food," said Edward.

"Okay. We'll eat, but then we have to go."

Savannah placed her purse in the empty chair and took a seat at one of the place settings. Edward brought piping-hot food over to the table and placed it in the center. Chloe came into the room. She wasn't her usual bubbly self as she gave her father a hug.

"Good morning, sweetheart," Edward said, and picked his daughter up. "How do you feel?"

She laid her head on his shoulder. He took a seat at the table, placed her on his knee.

"She's still feeling a little crappy," Savannah explained.

Edward touched her forehead. "She's still warm, too."

"I just gave her some Tylenol," Savannah said.

"Daddy made pancakes," Edward said. "Aren't you hungry?"

"No. I just want to lie down."

"Maybe she should just stay here," said Edward.

"She has a bed at home."

"I know she has a bed at home, but she has one here, too." Edward stood. "I'm going to tuck her back in."

Savannah sighed as he stepped out of the kitchen. He carried Chloe to her room and placed her in the bed, removed her shoes from her feet. Her head hit the pillow and she immediately closed her eyes. He kissed her forehead and pulled the covers over her. When he returned to the kitchen, Savannah had begun to make her plate.

"I have to get home, shower and change. Maybe I'll come back and pick her up a little later."

"Leave her. She's fine," Edward said. "Why don't you go home and grab some more clothes. Come back. We can fire up the barbecue grill later, cook some fish..."

"I don't know about that, Edward."

"I need to be near her. But I can't take care of her by myself when she's sick. I need your help."

Savannah cut her pancakes into little squares, and placed two pieces of turkey bacon on her plate. "Okay. I'll come back. But just for the night. We have church in the morning."

"Excellent." He sat down at the table across from her and made himself a healthy helping of pancakes and fruit.

He looked forward to her return.

With a baseball cap placed backward on his head and a chef's apron tied around his waist, he took a quick sip of his Heineken beer. Edward carefully flipped the thick fillets of mahimahi on the grill.

"So you two are just going to sit there lounging while I slave over a hot grill?"

"I made the fresh lemonade." Savannah smiled. Her legs were crossed and stretched across the lounge chair as she took a sip from her glass.

"And I helped Mommy." Chloe sat on the lounger next to her mother.

"Yes you did, sweet girl." Savannah toasted her glass against Chloe's plastic Doc McStuffins cup.

"Well, maybe you can come over here and help your dad cook this fish," said Edward.

Chloe giggled, and Savannah did, too.

"Oh, you think this is funny?" Edward placed the spatula down next to the grill and made his way over to Chloe, picked her up and slung her over his shoulder. He raced around the yard with her as she laughed heartily.

"Mommy, help me!" she exclaimed.

Savannah laughed and raised her glass in the air.

"Mommy can't help you now, kiddo." Edward continued to race around the yard. Then he placed Chloe into Savannah's lap. "Here, Mommy, help your daughter!"

He was beside himself with joy. He had his two favorite girls in one place for an entire evening and it felt good. He stepped into the house and grabbed a casserole dish to place the fish on. Went into the living room and found some music on his iPad. He played his Caribbean playlist and turned the volume up so that they could hear it in the backyard.

He peeked his head out the back door and asked Savannah, "Would you like a glass of wine?"

"I'd love one," she said.

He poured her a glass of Chardonnay, handed it to her.

"I would like a glass of wine, Daddy," said Chloe.

"And you will get one. In about twenty years." Edward laughed. "But until then, would you like another cup of lemonade, madam?"

"Yes," Chloe groaned.

He stepped into the kitchen. When his cell phone lit up, he walked over to the counter where it lay charging. He noticed a text message from Jack.

Call me when you have a minute. I have some news to share.

He made a mental note to call Jack once his phone was fully charged, poured Chloe a cup filled with lemonade and stepped back outside. The evening couldn't have been more perfect, with mild weather and palm trees blowing in the wind just before sunset. He glanced at Savannah lounging in her chair and noticed how beautiful she looked. Dressed in a pair of capri pants and a strapless shirt, her bare feet gave him the indication that she was comfortable.

"They're playing our song," he said to her.

As the lyrics of Gregory Isaacs's "Stranger in Town" drifted through the air, Edward remembered a time when he and Savannah loved each other.

"I love that song," she stated.

"Dance with me," he said.

"Edward, I don't feel like dancing..."

Before she could finish her protest, he'd already pulled her up from the lounger.

The two of them moved to the music, just as they had so many times before. He grabbed her hand and spun her around. He placed his hands on her small waist and got lost in the Caribbean rhythm that would forever be their song. As he pulled her close, he took in the moment.

While the nighttime drew near, the three of them enjoyed mahimahi and vegetables on a candlelit patio. Edward and Savannah laughed about the good times and told Chloe funny stories. After the mosquitoes began to bite, Savannah helped him take dishes into the house.

"I'm going to help Chloe get her bath," she told Edward. "She had a good afternoon, but she's feeling a little warm again."

"Okay, I'll finish cleaning up here."

Savannah and Chloe disappeared while Edward loaded dishes into the dishwasher. After he placed leftovers into plastic containers, he went into the living room. He found some soft music. Then he turned the television on ESPN, but muted it. He collapsed onto the leather sofa. Savannah returned and took a seat at the opposite end of the sofa, just as she had the night before. She wore a two-piece pajama set—a silky button-up shirt with matching shorts. Edward found it difficult to peel his eyes from her. The scent from whatever she'd bathed in caressed his nose.

Savannah stretched her feet onto the leather sofa. Edward moved closer and placed her feet on his lap, began to rub them. He squeezed her arches, heels and toes. She leaned her head back against the back of the sofa, closed her eyes. He knew she enjoyed the feel of his fingertips between her toes; she always had. He rubbed her ankles and then moved up to the calves of her bare legs.

"I remember those foot rubs, sensual and wonderful," she whispered.

He moved closer, placing her long legs in his lap. His fingers brushed against her face, caressed her chin. His breathing changed and his nose touched hers.

"I've missed you," he whispered.

She was silent, just stared into his eyes. He leaned in for her lips.

"Mommy." Chloe's voice startled them. She climbed onto the sofa, plopping herself between them.

"What's the matter, sweetheart?" Savannah asked.

"I can't sleep," Chloe whined. "Can I stay in here with you and Daddy?"

"Of course you can, baby." Edward said it, but wished his daughter's timing hadn't been so wrong.

He gathered himself, got his hormones under control. He hoped that once Chloe had fallen asleep, he could pick up where he left off with Savannah. He wanted to kiss her lips so badly. He tried not to let his desires overshadow his daughter's need to be near them. He tuned the television to the Disney Channel and gave Savannah a smile.

Soon Chloe's head rested against his chest, her eyes tightly shut.

"I think she's asleep," he whispered to a sleeping Savannah.

He carefully carried Chloe to her bedroom, tucked her into bed. When he returned to the den, he gently touched Savannah's shoulder. "Savannah," he whispered.

Her eyes opened slowly. "Yes."

"Why don't you go on to bed?"

She gave him a smile and then headed for the guest bedroom. Edward turned off the music, the television and the lights and headed to his bedroom. He took a quick shower and tried to rid himself of thoughts of his ex-wife and what he'd wanted to do with her before he was interrupted. He slipped into a pair of pajama pants, climbed into bed. He lay there in the darkness wondering what would have been had he kissed Savannah. The time he'd spent with her had been pleasurable, and he was grateful for it but didn't know where it was leading, if anywhere. She was leaving the country soon. However, he couldn't help thinking that he'd never stopped loving her. A wave of familiar emotions suddenly flooded in, and he wondered if she'd ever stopped loving him.

Sunday morning, and Savannah had obviously forgotten all about church because she was still there, and still wearing those sexy silky pajamas. He tried not to stare, but couldn't help wondering what it would feel like if he slipped his fingertips beneath those silky shorts. Thoughts like that had plagued him all night, and he hadn't been able to shake them.

By the afternoon, the trio had found themselves strolling along Jupiter Beach. Edward lifted Chloe onto his shoulders. Savannah carried a picnic basket filled with California rolls, a fresh garden salad, a bottle of chilled wine, and a small bottle of fruit juice for Chloe. After finding the perfect spot, they stretched their oversize beach towels out onto the sand. Edward opened the bottle of wine with a corkscrew and poured it into wineglasses. Then he opened the bottle of fruit juice and handed it to Chloe. It was these times that he missed with Savannah—simple Sunday afternoons on the beach, away from the static of the world. The beach was where he and Savannah had planned their lives together—their next steps, their wedding.

After stopping by Savannah's for a change of clothing and picking up Edward's car from his office, they ended up at his home again. He didn't know how he did it, but he'd managed to convince her to spend yet another night. Chloe rushed into her bedroom, and Savannah took her business suit and overnight bag to the guest bedroom. Edward headed for the shower to wash the sand from his legs and feet.

The weekend had been enlightening. It felt good to have his family underneath one roof, even if it was short-lived. He began to toss the what-ifs around in his head. What if he could convince Savannah to stay in the country? What if he could have her back in his life, his home, his bed? What if he had never lost her in the first place? He washed his hair and his chest before stepping out of the shower.

As Savannah stood in the kitchen cutting into the flesh of a watermelon that they'd picked up at the market, Edward crept up from behind, wrapped his arms tightly around her waist. He planted a trail of kisses onto her neck. He hoped he hadn't overstepped his bounds, but he needed to feel her in his arms. She turned to face him, wrapped her arms around his neck. His lips touched hers, and he kissed her shamelessly. Finally and deeply.

"I've wanted to do that all weekend," he whispered.

"And I've wanted you to."

Edward's emotions and hormones ran rampant. There were so many things he wanted to say, but didn't know how to put them into sentences. Instead he just held her close. Besides, it was too soon for her to know all the things he'd been thinking—it was best to keep his thoughts to himself. She didn't need to know that he had thought of her every single day since she'd left, and had actually contemplated ways of winning her back. She didn't need to know that he had beat himself up about losing her, and that he hadn't found anyone who made him feel the way she had. He had managed to find something wrong with every single beautiful woman who had crossed his path, and he hadn't understood why until now. His hand moved from the center of her back and caressed the roundness of her behind.

She pulled away from his embrace.

“What’s wrong?” he asked.

“Too much, too soon.” She wiped his kisses from the corners of her mouth in a slow downward motion.

“I’m sorry. I just thought…”

“I’m going to check on Chloe,” she said and then left the kitchen without another word.

Edward exhaled, leaned his back against the granite island. He’d blown it with her—been too hasty. He’d been thinking with the wrong head.

Chapter 8

"What the hell do you mean, you spent the weekend with Edward?"

"Shhh." Savannah pressed a finger against her lips, a wide grin on her face. She walked around her desk and shut the door. "I don't want everyone in the entire office to know."

When Maia first met Savannah in art school, she was going through the divorce with Edward. Maia had been the one to observe her during the most vulnerable time of her life.

"What was that about?"

"Chloe was sick, and we were caring for her...*together*."

"What else were you doing *together*?"

"Nothing!" Savannah couldn't help blushing.

"You're lying," said Maia. "Girl, you are blushing."

"No seriously. Nothing happened."

"Not even a kiss?" Maia asked.

Savannah smiled. Averted her eyes from her friend's.

"You kissed him!" Maia laughed. "Savannah, what is going on? Just last week you were taking his ass to court because he was giving you a hard time about leaving the country with Chloe."

"I know," said Savannah.

"Now you're playing house with him?" Maia asked.

"It was unexpected. Chloe got sick. Edward showed up at the hospital. He needed a ride home. Things just sort of happened."

"You still love him, don't you?"

"I'll be the first to admit that I have unresolved feelings for Edward. I need closure if I'm ever going to move to London."

"Well, you won't get closure by spending the weekend at his house. You're setting yourself up. He had his chance with you, sweetie, and he blew it. I say chalk it up as a loss and move on."

Savannah paced the floor. "I've been thinking. Maybe I can pull back the petition…just for a little while."

"Oh no," Maia groaned.

"Just temporarily…"

"Haven't you already filed it?"

"Yes, but if I call the courthouse, maybe I can intercept it before Edward is served today."

"Savannah!"

"I'm not saying that I won't file the petition. I just want to hold off until…"

"Until what, honey? Until he breaks your heart again?"

"You're being so cynical."

"I'm a realist. I'm that friend who tells you the truth when others won't." Maia stood, walked toward the door and opened it. She quickly switched the conversation. "So are we doing Chinese for lunch or what?"

"Chinese is fine." Savannah searched the internet for the phone number of the Palm Beach County Courthouse.

"Fine," Maia said. "And Savannah…"

Savannah was busy jotting the phone number on a sticky note.

"Savannah Carrington!"

"Yes, Maia."

"Just be careful, honey." Maia held both hands over her chest.

"I will." Savannah gave Maia a gentle smile, one that let her friend know that she need not worry.

As soon as the door was pulled shut, Savannah picked up the phone and dialed the phone number. She attempted to work her way through the teleprompts to get to a live person, and quickly grew frustrated and impatient. Didn't they know she'd had a change of heart? The weekend with Edward had been unexpected, and caused her to rethink things. He'd kissed her with those soft, delectable lips that she remembered all too well. He'd wrapped those strong arms around her so tightly, and his tongue had explored the inside of her mouth causing a tingle between her thighs. She'd wanted him, but her good sense told her to run away.

After being placed on hold for the third time, she hung up the phone. Holding the receiver against her chin, she flipped through the internet again.

After a light tap on the door, Jarrod walked in without invitation. "Are you free for lunch?"

"Plans with Maia."

"Cancel them. We're celebrating."

"Celebrating what?"

"Are you serious right now?" he asked.

She *was* serious. And distracted. She didn't have time for Jarrod's riddles. And he was becoming increasingly annoying.

"I'm serious, Jarrod. And I'm really busy right now," she said. "So if you don't mind…"

He moved closer, came around to her side of the desk.

He grabbed the telephone receiver from her hand and hung it up.

"It's my birthday," he said softly.

"Oh, Jarrod. I completely forgot." She smiled. "Happy birthday."

He grabbed her and pretended to dance to imaginary music.

"Let's go dancing after work." His lips brushed against her earlobe.

She didn't even see Edward as he appeared in her doorway. By the time she saw him, he was standing on the opposite side of her desk. He threw a yellow envelope onto her desk.

"I was served with your petition today. At my office of all places," he said. "I guess you're still going through with this…this ridiculous idea of moving to London and taking Chloe with you."

"Edward… I…" She pulled away from Jarrod's embrace.

"I hope you're happy!" He said, "It sure looks like you are."

"This is not what it looks like, Edward."

"I don't really care. I just care about my daughter. If you want a fight, I'll give you one. I'll see you in court!"

She plopped down and sank into her leather chair. She was speechless. She'd had a change of heart, at least for the moment—only Edward didn't know it. Their weekend together had somehow penetrated her soul, had her reconsidering her idea of moving away. She'd spent the entire night thinking about Edward and wondering if there was any hope of reconciliation. But now…

"Jarrod, I know it's your birthday, but I'm sorry, I can't have lunch with you today. Or go dancing with you this evening."

"Are you seeing him again?"

"No."

"Because I know how much he hurt you before." Jarrod moved to the other side of her desk and went toward the door. "I wouldn't want him hurting you again."

"You don't have to worry."

"Good. I'll take a rain check on lunch and dancing." He pointed a finger at her. "This time."

She exhaled when he finally left and pulled the door shut behind him. She covered her face with both hands.

Zumba was a challenge, particularly since exercising was the last thing that Savannah wanted to do. But she was committed to the class. She danced to the sounds of Pitbull as she attempted to keep up with her energetic instructor. She and Maia had splurged on fried chicken instead of Chinese food for lunch, and she needed to burn the extra calories.

Maia grinned at Savannah and wiggled her behind to the music.

"Snap out of it, chica!" Maia yelled over the music.

"I can't. I'm torn."

"You said it yourself. Your mother needs you, and it's time you did something for yourself anyway. Isn't that what you said?"

"I know it's what I said, Maia, but it's not that simple now."

"It *is* that simple. Edward had his chance to have his family around, and he threw it all away for a campaign that didn't even pan out."

"He could've won," Savannah defended him. "In fact he only lost by a small margin."

"Defensive, aren't we?" Maia giggled. "Had he kept his focus on the campaign and not on that beautiful little campaign manager, things might've turned out different."

Savannah ignored Maia's comments and continued to sway her hips to the music. She'd thought the same thing in the past—that Edward and Quinn had been much too close for her comfort, but she would never admit it to Maia.

Savannah tossed her gym bag over her shoulder as she bid Maia a good-night. "I'll see you tomorrow, girl."

"Take care, Savannah." Maia, with a pink baseball cap backward on her head, waved and headed toward her two-door coupe.

Savannah sat in the driver's seat of her Toyota, checked her cell phone for missed calls. Edward had called and then texted—I'm sorry about barging into your office today. I was out of line.

"Apology accepted." She didn't hesitate to call back and tell him that. "Edward, I'm sorry. I tried calling the courthouse to at least delay the petition."

"Have you had a change of heart?"

"I don't know what my heart is feeling right now, but until I'm sure, I want to delay it."

"Listen. This weekend I'm headed to the islands. It's my parents' wedding anniversary, and they're having this big celebration at the Grove. My parents would love to see Chloe...and you, of course. You know they still love you very much..." he said. "Anyway, you don't have to give me an answer now. Sleep on it, and let me know sometime this week."

Savannah was silent. Didn't know what to say. He'd caught her off guard.

"Okay."

"I think it would be a great opportunity for Chloe to see my parents before the two of you head off to London...if that's what you decide to do."

"Edward, I..."

"Just think about it and let me know."

She didn't need to think about it. She'd already made

her decision, but she told him, “I love your parents. I’ll let you know.”

“Great. Sooner is better so that I can purchase tickets.”

“I’ll sleep on it. Call you in the morning.”

She would make him sweat, at least for the night. And tomorrow she’d go shopping for a party dress for her former in-laws’ anniversary party.

Chapter 9

As the jet soared above the clouds, Chloe closed her eyes and held on tightly to Edward's hand.

"We're almost there, baby."

He glanced over at Savannah. Her head was leaned against the back of the seat, and her eyes were closed tightly also. He suddenly remembered her fear of flying as well. He reached over Chloe and touched Savannah's shoulder. She opened her eyes and gave him a warm smile. He massaged her neck and shoulder and tried to help her relax. He held on to both of them until the wheels of the jet finally hit the pavement.

The Bahamas was a beautiful eighty-six degrees, and Edward breathed in the fresh smell of the ocean. He loved his home and visited frequently. The three of them sat in the backseat of a taxicab as the driver took them to his family's B and B. As the car pulled up in front of the Grove, Edward pulled twenty-five dollars in Bahamian currency from his pocket and handed it to the driver. He usually held on to his Bahamian dollars for his frequent visits to the islands.

"Thank you, sir," he told the driver before ushering Savannah and Chloe out of the vehicle. "Keep the change."

"Thank you," said the Bahamian driver as he popped the trunk and assisted with their luggage.

Savannah admired the architecture of the historical homes that had been transformed into a B and B. There were three of them, lined along the ocean right there together. She thought they were beautiful and elegant, and she couldn't wait to see the inside. Edward struggled with their bags.

"Well, well, well, if it isn't Edward Talbot," said Jasmine as they approached the lobby. "Oh my God, Savannah, is that you?"

"Jazzy!" Savannah gave Edward's sister a strong hug.

"You look so gorgeous, as always." Jasmine smiled genuinely. "And who's this little lady? This can't be little Chloe!"

Edward hugged his sister. "This is Chloe. Chloe, say hello to our Aunt Jasmine."

"Call me Aunt Jazzy."

"Hi, Aunt Jazzy," Chloe said softly.

Jasmine, with her long natural hair and perfectly sized body; it was no wonder she'd snagged a few modeling gigs while living in L.A. She grabbed Chloe in her arms and kissed her cheek. "You're so pretty. I don't think I've seen you since you were in diapers."

Savannah remembered the time that Edward's mother and sisters had come for a visit, just a few days after she'd given birth to Chloe. They'd been helpful—preparing meals, cleaning house and changing soiled diapers. They'd kept a watchful eye on Chloe while Savannah slept. It was during that visit that she'd fallen in love with them.

Although Edward traveled back and forth between the islands on business, he hadn't had a chance to take Chloe along. He'd had intentions of it, but the time never seemed right. He regretted not allowing her to connect with his family, but now was as good a time as any.

"It's been such a long time, Jazzy. So good to see you. You look great."

All of Edward's sisters had been fond of Savannah. They all loved her like family, and that hadn't changed with the divorce. In fact, Edward had been concerned that if he'd brought someone new home, he'd have trouble with the women in his family.

"Where is everybody?" Edward asked.

"Alyson and Samson are flying in from Miami later tonight. Nate got in last night. Whitney's flying in from Texas tomorrow morning, and Denny will be here tomorrow night. That's everybody."

"Great. Everyone will be here for the celebration," said Edward. "Where are our quarters?"

"I have you set up in the Symonette Room," Jasmine said.

"And Savannah?"

"Oh, you're not sharing quarters?" Jasmine smiled.

"No," Savannah interjected. "Chloe and I will need a separate room, thank you."

"Oh, I wasn't aware of that. I'll have to check and see if we have an extra room available. We're pretty tight this weekend."

"Are you kidding? I told you I was coming," Edward said.

"Right! You told me that *you* were coming." Jasmine walked over to the front desk, logged on to the computer. "Just give me a second."

"This is a bit inconvenient," Savannah whispered to Edward. "Perhaps Chloe and I can bunk at your parents' home."

"She'll find us something," Edward assured her. "Don't worry."

Jasmine looked up from the computer. "I don't have one single room available, guys. I'm sorry. Everything's booked for the entire weekend."

Edward sighed. "You and Chloe can take the Symonette Room. I'll bunk at my parents' for the weekend."

"I can try to find you a rollaway bed, big brother. How about that?" Jasmine asked.

Edward shrugged. "I'm going to stay at our home in Governor's Harbour."

"The Symonette Room is one of our more spacious rooms. And it has the best view. Quite romantic, too." She cleared her throat. "Should be plenty of space for the three of you."

"I'm sure my old room at home will do just fine." Edward gathered the luggage.

"Okay, suit yourself." Jasmine moved from behind the desk, reached her hand out to Chloe. "And you, young lady…how about you come with me? I spotted some ice cream in the freezer earlier today. Would you like some?"

"Yes!" Chloe exclaimed.

"And we'll have to do something about this hair." Jasmine ran her hand across Chloe's thick mane. "Maybe some plaits."

"That would be nice," Savannah said, laughing. "I don't know what to do with Chloe's hair! It's just a thick bush."

"It's okay. Auntie Jazzy will take care of it." Jasmine grabbed Chloe's hand and headed for the kitchen. "Let's go for ice cream."

Savannah and Edward climbed the wooden, refinished stairs to the Symonette Room.

"I'm sorry that I won't be staying on Harbour Island with you and Chloe for the weekend, but I'll be just a phone call away. I swear this wasn't preplanned. I thought Jazzy understood that we would need separate rooms."

"It's okay. We'll make the best of it." Savannah walked over to the window and took in the view. "Very nice. This place is awesome. It's much more than I'd imagined."

"I can't take the credit. Jasmine and her husband, Jackson, spearheaded the entire project."

"It's so hard to believe that Jazzy is married now. I still see her as your baby sister. She's all grown up."

"And Jackson is a good man. He's one of my best friends, so I don't have to worry about her."

"Good." Savannah smiled. "Because we all know that you're a worrier."

"I'm not a worrier, I just like to protect the people that I love."

"You can't save everyone," Savannah said.

"I'll sure try," Edward said. "I think we should head over to Governor's Harbour to my parents' house. I'm sure they're anxious to see Chloe."

"I'm sure they are," said Savannah. "I just need to freshen up a bit."

"Fine. I'm going to walk the property a bit and visit with Jazzy. Just let me know when you're ready."

"Okay, I'll meet you in the lobby."

Edward's childhood home smelled of Bahamian spices. He loved coming home. Although he enjoyed living in Florida, there was nothing like his home on the islands. A place where he and his five other siblings were reared. Edward was born in Key West, but the family moved to Eleuthera when he was a small boy. His parents moved to the islands to care for his ailing grandfather.

Edward, the oldest of the bunch, was a precocious young man. His father, Paul John, had hopes that his oldest son would follow in his professional footsteps and study medicine, but Edward had plans of his own. He was more interested in law and politics and had already immersed himself in an upcoming local election by the time he'd graduated from Harvard. Changing the laws was just as dear to Edward's heart as being a father.

Edward and his siblings had inherited three historical homes from their grandparents, which had been transformed into the B and B on Harbour Island. Even after the Grove was completed and operational, Edward still had no intention of moving back to the islands to help run it. However, he'd been instrumental in the renovation and obtaining funding for the family's business. He was happy that his sister Jasmine had taken a lead in making the Grove the extraordinary property that it was. It had quickly become one of the most sought-after properties on Harbour Island, which was why there weren't any vacancies for his weekend visit with Savannah and Chloe.

"Where is everybody?" Edward asked loudly.

"Oh my goodness, Edward Talbot! You're here." His mother, Beverly, rushed from the kitchen wiping her hands on the end of her apron. "Oh, my! Who is this little young lady?"

Beverly Talbot was an older version of Edward's sister, Whitney, with medium brown skin and a slender body that didn't represent that of a middle-aged woman. Wisdom hid behind those eyes, and her smile was the same one that Edward owned.

"This is Chloe." Edward grinned with pride. She'd been his greatest achievement. "Chloe, give your grandmother a hug."

"Oh, you're just so precious." Beverly gave the girl a tight squeeze. "And Savannah, you're just as pretty as I remember."

Savannah embraced Edward's mother. "Hello, Mrs. Talbot. So good to see you."

"I believe you used to call me Mother. That still works just fine for me." Beverly placed her hand on Savannah's cheek. "So, the three of you will be staying here, yes?"

"No, Mother, just me," Edward interjected. "Savannah and Chloe will be staying at the Grove."

"What!" said Beverly.

Paul John Talbot came into the room wearing a pair of dingy coveralls and carrying a wrench. "I heard the voice of a little person in the house."

"Pop, what are you fixing on now?"

"Bathroom sink is clogged," Paul John stated. "And you must be Chloe. They told me they were sending someone to help me with the plumbing. Are you the help?"

Chloe grinned and shook her head no.

"No? You mean you don't know how to fix the bathroom sink?"

Chloe shook her head again.

"Well, then. I guess I'll have to do it myself." He pretended to walk away and then turned back to Chloe. "Can you fix anything?"

"Um." Chloe placed a finger against her cheek. "My Barbie's arm came off one time and I fixed it."

"Well, there you go! That qualifies you to fix a sink then."

Chloe shrugged her shoulders. "Okay."

"Say hello to your grandfather, Chloe," said Edward.

Paul John gave his granddaughter a handshake, then turned to Savannah. "Good seeing you, Savannah. I'd hug you, but I'm much too dirty."

"Good seeing you, too, Mr. Talbot." Savannah giggled.

"You all must be hungry," Beverly said. "Come on into the kitchen and get something to eat."

Savannah and Chloe followed Beverly into the kitchen, while Edward took his bags down the hall to his old bedroom. The room was just as it always was when he visited home, with fresh linen on the bed and his favorite chocolates in a candy dish on the dresser. He opened the drapes and let some sunshine in, unpacked his bag. When he finished he made his way into the kitchen where Savannah and Chloe were scarfing down fish and grits.

"Where's Nate? Jazzy told me he's here," Edward said to his mother.

"Nate's already up and running about the island. You know he's not one to sit still for too long."

"Right. He might be at the beach catching some waves on his board."

"Maybe," Beverly said. "Why don't you sit down and have a bite to eat, son?"

Edward didn't waste any time fixing a plate and sitting down at the kitchen table across from Savannah. He listened while she chitchatted with his mother, and suddenly his mind wandered. He wondered how he had allowed Savannah to slip away. His mother had always had her opinions about everyone, but she'd loved Savannah genuinely. His entire family had embraced her in the past, and it was clear that she was still very dear to them. Even his sister Alyson, who was fond of very few people, loved Savannah.

"Is anybody home?" the voice in the living room asked, and then Alyson appeared in the doorway of the kitchen. She'd lost a few extra pounds since Edward had last seen her. Marriage had done her well. Though she struggled with her weight, she was still just as beautiful as all the Talbot women. "You're all in here feeding your faces!"

"Hello, dear. We didn't hear you," Beverly said.

"Obviously." Alyson walked over and kissed her mother's

cheek. "Oh my goodness, Savannah! You look fabulous. What are you doing here? You and Edward back together again?"

Savannah stood and gave Alyson a strong hug. "It's good to see you, Alyson. And no, we're not."

"Did I miss something, big brother?" Alyson blew Edward a kiss.

"You haven't missed anything. I just wanted everyone to see Chloe...and she's been a little under the weather, so I invited Savannah along to help me look after her."

"Didn't you get married recently?" Alyson asked Savannah.

"No," Savannah said sweetly. "I was engaged, but things didn't quite work out for us."

"Well, that must've been good news for you, big brother." Alyson grinned at Edward and then turned to Savannah. "He was beside himself with grief when he thought another man was going to take you away. Showed up on my doorstep."

"Alyson!" Beverly exclaimed. "Behave."

"What, Mother? You know it's true." Alyson kept going. "I thought I was going to have to give him a sedative."

"You just don't know when to quit, do you?" asked Edward.

Alyson rolled her eyes, ignored his question. "And this must be my beautiful niece."

"Yes, this is Chloe," Savannah stated.

Alyson squeezed Chloe's shoulders.

"Where is my brother-in-law?" Edward asked. "He needs to come and get you under control."

"From what?" Alyson giggled. "Samson's getting our bags out of the car."

"I'm right here!" Samson exclaimed. "Is she misbehaving again?"

"As always." Edward stood and gave Samson a strong handshake. "Good to see you, bro."

"Likewise," said Samson as he moved around the table to Beverly and kissed her cheek. "Mother, good to see you."

Beverly placed her palm against Samson's face. "Are you hungry?"

"Famished, Mother."

Beverly shook her head and looked at Alyson. "You have to feed this man, dear."

"Samson knew I was a busy woman before he married me," Alyson said.

"So because you're busy, he can't eat?" asked Edward. "Is that what you're saying?"

"Mind your business, Edward," Alyson warned.

"Like you minded yours earlier?" Edward asked.

"It's certainly not that she can't cook," Beverly said. "I taught them all very well."

"It's that she won't," Edward mumbled.

"Okay, okay," said Alyson. "It's true. I don't cook that often. However, Samson is a pretty good cook himself, so we get by."

Edward ignored Alyson and turned to Samson. "Samson, this is Savannah, by the way. Savannah, meet Alyson's husband, Samson. I honestly don't know how he puts up with her."

"Pleased to meet you." Savannah giggled and reached her hand out to Samson. "I didn't know that you got married, Alyson."

"Yeah, it wasn't a big to-do. Just a little justice of the peace type of thing."

"She refused to do it the right way. She knows the Talbots are a celebratory bunch," said Beverly. "We were looking forward to a big to-do."

"You know I don't like making a big fuss of things. Spending all sorts of unnecessary money."

"We can still have that beautiful ceremony…whenever you want, Alyson," said Samson.

"No need." Alyson grinned and held her hand out to show Savannah her ring. "This rock is beautiful enough."

"It is. Very beautiful." Savannah smiled. "Congratulations to you both."

Alyson waved her hand in the air to brush off the sentiment.

"Thank you," Samson interjected. "A pleasure meeting you, Savannah."

"And this is our daughter, Chloe," Edward said.

Chloe was a mixture of Edward and Savannah, but more Edward. She had his smile and his long, slender frame. With thick hair and bright, inquisitive eyes, she had the ability to charm everyone around her.

"Well, aren't you beautiful." Samson smiled and then took Chloe's small hand in his, kissed the back of it. He removed his fedora from his head, turned to Alyson. "I'm going to drop the bags in our room. Can you fix me a plate?"

"Yes, can you at least fix the man a plate?" Edward instigated. "And I'd like a cold beer while you're headed that way."

Alyson groaned, but then gave Samson a gentle smile. "Of course, sweetheart."

When she handed Edward a beer, he smiled. He loved being at his childhood home. He glanced at Savannah and Chloe. There was nothing more important than family.

Chapter 10

Contemporary Caribbean music and laughter filled the Talbot home. Edward crossed one leg over the other, reclined in the easy chair in the corner of the room and took a sip of his wine. Denny peeked his head in the screen door, a wide grin on his face.

"Oh my word!" Beverly exclaimed. "What are you doing here?"

"I can leave if you'd like." Denny gave his mother a wicked grin and then removed his duffel bag from his shoulder and set it down.

"Get in here, boy!" Beverly demanded. "I didn't even know you were coming."

"I thought I would surprise you. That's why I swore Jazzy to secrecy." Denny hugged his mother tightly and kissed her cheek.

"And she was able to keep that secret?" Edward asked.

"I guess so. Mother didn't know I was coming."

"Good to see you, young man!" Edward grabbed his brother in a headlock.

"Hello, Savannah." Denny gave her a warm smile while

being playfully choked by Edward. "Surprised to see you here."

"Hello, Denny. I can't believe you're all grown up now." Savannah sat on the sofa next to Chloe, her hand resting beneath the bowl of her wineglass. "You were just a young boy the last time I saw you."

"Are you and this old guy back together?"

"No!" Edward and Savannah said it in unison.

"Okay! I was just trying to figure out what was going on here." He moved from Edward's grasp and then turned to Chloe and smiled. "You must be Chloe. I'm your Uncle Denny."

"Hi," Chloe said softly.

Denny turned to his oldest sister. "Alyson, good to see you."

"You're not AWOL, are you?" Alyson asked with a raised eyebrow.

"Of course not." He kissed his sister's cheek and then shook Samson's hand. "I'm on leave."

"Good to see you, Denny," said Samson.

"Hey, Pop." Denny hugged his father, after which he went back to the door and opened it just a bit wider. A young woman followed him inside. "Everybody, this is Gabrielle. Gabby for short."

"Hi." Gabby was dressed in military fatigues, her hair in a ponytail and a cap on her head. She gave the family a slight wave of her hand.

Everyone was too shocked to speak.

"Hello, Gabby." Paul John Talbot was the first to say something and shook her hand.

"Does Sage know that you're home?" Alyson asked Denny about his high school sweetheart, the girl he'd vowed to marry as soon as he returned from boot camp.

"I haven't spoken with her," Denny said nonchalantly.

"Have you introduced Sage to Gabby?" Alyson continued.

"No, Alyson, I haven't!"

"It's very nice meeting you, Gabby," said Beverly Talbot. "Why don't you come in and have a seat?"

"So, obviously you're on the force, too," Edward stated. "Did you train with the navy SEALs as well?"

"Yes, sir, I did," Gabby said.

"Sir?" Edward said. "She called me sir."

"Because you're old," Denny said. "She's respecting her elders."

"Watch it, boy."

"Gabby's from San Diego, California," Denny exclaimed.

"You're a long way from home, aren't you?" Alyson asked. "How did you wind up in the Bahamas, and with my baby brother…who is engaged?"

"You're engaged?" Gabby turned to Denny.

"Not anymore," Denny stated, and then through clenched teeth said, "Alyson, please."

"You're not engaged to Sage anymore?" Beverly asked. "When did that change?"

"I haven't quite told her." Denny became uncomfortable. He grabbed his brother by the arm. "Edward, can I see you in the kitchen for a minute?"

Edward followed Denny into the kitchen.

"Are you telling me that you haven't broken things off with Sage?" Edward whispered.

"I didn't know how to tell her in a letter or over the phone that I'm seeing Gabby now," said Denny.

"I have to tell you, you did that all wrong, boy!" Edward said. "You can't bring a new girl home when you haven't told your old girl that she's been dumped. I thought you loved Sage."

"I do… I mean I did." Denny rubbed his head in frustration. "It's just that I finally got away from the Bahamas for the first time…and there were just so many options."

"Girls everywhere, huh?" Edward smiled.

"Everywhere! Have you seen Gabby?"

"She's cute," Edward admitted. "But Sage is a good girl. She deserves to be treated so much better. She at least needs to know that she's been replaced. You should know better."

"You're judging me?" Denny asked. "The way you treated Savannah?"

"I admit, I wasn't the best husband. But I regret losing her. There! I said it," Edward admitted. "I regret losing her. I needed to hear myself say it aloud."

It was the first time he'd admitted it to someone other than himself.

"You're serious? You still love Savannah."

Edward shrugged his shoulders. Didn't admit or deny loving Savannah. "All I know is when you find a good woman, you should do everything in your power to keep her."

Denny sat at the kitchen table, frustration on his face. "Gabby has so much to offer. She's beautiful, ambitious…"

"Sage is just as beautiful. Maybe not as ambitious, but the grass isn't always greener on the other side, Denny," said Edward. He patted him on the shoulder. "You got your hands full, boy."

"What should I do?" he asked, and grabbed Edward, who was trying to leave the kitchen.

"I don't know. What do you want?"

"I want them both."

"Boy, you're losing it," Edward said. "This is a recipe for disaster."

"I know." Denny sighed.

"If I were you, I'd go rescue Gabby. Your sister can be a beast."

"You're right." Denny stood quickly and rushed into the living room where Alyson had already started giving Gabby the third degree.

Edward shook his head and hoped that his brother made it out of his predicament unharmed, but he wasn't confident that he would. He took a look at his watch. "I think I should get you and Chloe back to the Grove," he told Savannah.

Savannah smiled and stood.

"I'll drive you to the water ferry," his father offered.

"Thanks, Pop. That would be great," Edward said as he leaned in and kissed his mother's cheek. "I'll be back shortly. Just want to get these ladies to their room safe and sound."

"Should I wait up?" his mother asked.

"No. Don't worry too much. I'll call you when I'm headed back," he promised.

"Fine. I'll save you some coconut cake."

"That would be nice."

He gave his brother one final cautionary glance before walking out onto the front porch.

At the Grove, he carried Chloe up the stairs. Her head rested against his shoulder. She'd fallen asleep on the short drive from the water taxi to the Grove. Savannah unlocked the door to their room and Edward gently laid Chloe onto the queen-size bed. He removed her shoes and then kissed her forehead. He stepped out onto the balcony and gazed at the stars. Savannah followed.

"It's a beautiful night," he told her.

"It is. And this is a beautiful place. Thank you for inviting me," she told him.

"My pleasure."

"It was so good seeing everybody."

"They all still love you very much."

"And I them." She smiled at him. "Poor Denny. What's he going to do with two women?"

"What do you mean, poor Denny? He got himself into this mess." Edward chuckled. "And now he's got to figure his way out of it."

"He's young and foolish," she said.

"Yes! He's going to learn the hard way what it means to lose someone he loves. He'll regret it for the rest of his life."

"You sound like an authority on the matter."

"I am." He looked at her. "I lost you."

For a brief, uncomfortable moment she was silent, and he wished she would say something.

"I think we both sort of lost each other," she finally resolved.

His fingertips brushed against her face and he moved closer, waited for her to stop him, but she didn't. He wrapped his arms around her shoulders, pulled her into him. His nose gently touched hers, and then his lips kissed hers. She wrapped her arms around his waist, caressed his back. As the waves from the ocean crashed against the shore, his tongue danced against her mint-flavored mouth.

He still loved her. He knew it, and so did the universe.

Chapter 11

Savannah opened her eyes and noticed the moonlight as it reflected against the wall. Edward's arms were wrapped tightly around her waist, and she breathed in his cologne. His chin rested against her neck as light snores escaped from his lips. He'd fallen asleep right there, and she moved closer into him, snuggled closer.

They'd talked until the wee hours of the morning until they were both too tired to continue the conversation. They talked about what their relationship had been and where they'd both gone wrong. They'd become reacquainted in a matter of hours. Conversations like this one had never occurred in their marriage. He'd been too busy nurturing his career. And she'd given up on them much too soon. He'd needed her more than she ever knew.

After they'd both grown tired of talking and gazing at the stars from the balcony, Edward decided to stay on Harbour Island.

"It's late, and the water ferry isn't running any more tonight. Maybe I can just crash in that chair in the corner," he'd said.

"Or maybe you can just snuggle with us here in the bed. There's plenty of room," Savannah had suggested.

And so he did. He'd kicked his Dockers casual shoes from his feet and stretched across the bed. She'd taken a quick shower and changed into a pair of knit pajamas with the shortest of shorts. When she came back into the room Edward had removed his shirt and was relaxed, eyes closed as he listened to Caribbean music on his iPhone. She climbed into bed between him and Chloe. He smiled and then turned off the lamp. She'd rested her head against his chest, and he held her tightly.

Now she was awake, taking in the moment. She felt safe in his arms—as though she still belonged there. As though she had never left them. She closed her eyes, pulled his arms tighter around her and intertwined her fingers with his.

Morning came suddenly, it seemed, and she felt alarmed as if she'd overslept. She felt the empty bed next to her. Edward was gone, and so was Chloe. When they both came through the door carrying breakfast—a tray filled with an omelet, fresh fruit and a glass of freshly squeezed orange juice—Savannah sat up in the bed.

"What is all of this?" she asked.

"We brought you breakfast, Mommy!" Chloe exclaimed.

"Yes, you did," Savannah said. "It looks delicious."

"Raquel cooked it," said Chloe.

"Raquel?" Savannah glanced at Edward.

"The Grove's cook." He set the tray on her lap. "She's the best."

"Aunt Jazzy was downstairs, too," Chloe said. "She's taking me shopping and to the market today."

"Oh, she is?" Savannah smiled at her daughter.

Edward interjected, “I told Jasmine it was okay to spend the day with Chloe. Are you okay with that?”

“Of course.”

“Good. Because I thought you and I would go sailing. My cousin Stephen has a powerboat and I have something I want to show you,” he said. “So eat up and then get dressed.”

Savannah smiled at the thought of a surprise. She noticed that Edward was wearing fresh clothing. “You changed clothes.”

“Pop brought my suitcase over this morning.”

“Well, that was sweet of him,” said Savannah. “Your father is a gem.”

“The apple doesn’t fall far from the tree,” Edward boasted.

“You’re right.” Savannah smiled, then had a sip of her orange juice, took a forkful of her omelet. “I’ll be quick.”

They traveled across the ocean as Edward’s cousin Stephen steered his powerboat, *Sophia*. He was quite fond of her, and used her to transport tourists back and forth across the ocean. It was how he made his living—giving people memorable experiences. And when Edward had called him for a favor, he was happy to oblige. She liked Stephen. He had a gentle spirit with a bright smile. She thought he would’ve been a perfect catch for her friend Maia. Someone to tame her. It was their first time meeting, but before long, he and Savannah seemed like old friends.

Savannah took in the beautiful turquoise waters. She could actually see the rainbow of fish species as they swam beneath the clear water. She reclined on the leather seat in the port of the boat, while Edward relaxed in its bow and chatted with his cousin. The wind brushed against her face, and her shades shielded her eyes from the sunshine.

She wore a two-piece yellow bikini underneath her mesh cover-up. A smile danced in the corner of her mouth as she watched Edward.

She took in the curve of his chin and his strong jaw. Those lips that she'd spent the evening kissing only hours ago. His strong arms that had wrapped tightly around her as they gazed at the moon from their ocean-side patio. Her heart had fluttered, something that hadn't happened since the first time Edward's lips met hers—long before they were married. Back then she'd fallen for him quickly and hard. They were both hopeless romantics. It was another thing they had in common.

Stephen started to navigate the boat to shore, toward a private island in the middle of nowhere.

"Where are we?" Savannah asked.

"My little hidden jewel." Edward gave her a wide grin.

"You mean my little hidden jewel," said Stephen.

"Can I just have this moment, please?" asked Edward, and then with a lowered voice said, "I'm trying to impress the lady here."

Stephen lifted his hands in surrender and then turned to Savannah. "It's his little hidden jewel."

"Well, whomever it belongs to, it's beautiful." Savannah smiled.

Stephen dropped an anchor to steady the boat and then climbed out. He assisted Edward as he disembarked from the boat. Edward grabbed Savannah by the waist and lifted her out. She pressed her body against his to balance herself, and her face met his for a moment. Her feet gently touched the sand, and he let her go. Edward grabbed a backpack and a red cooler from the boat and carried them to shore.

"Follow me," he told Savannah.

"I have a family that I need to pick up and take back to

Harbour Island. I'll be back shortly," said Stephen. "Enjoy your time here."

"Okay, man," Edward said.

"He's leaving us?" Savannah asked as she rushed to catch up with Edward.

"We'll be fine." The confident Edward grabbed her by the hand.

She followed, her nerves easing just a little bit more with each step. Edward's confidence was one of the things that she loved about him. He had the ability to allay her fears.

Seagulls tiptoed along the island's coast and thousands of little baby crabs played hide-and-seek in the sand. Edward grabbed wood and placed it on an old grill, started a fire. He pulled fresh fish, lobsters and shrimp from the red cooler and placed them on the grill. He chopped fresh onions, potatoes and mangoes and seasoned them with a Bahamian rub, then placed them on the grill. He set the cooler on an old picnic table.

"Where did you get all of that?"

"Stephen is a diver and caught the fish. He bought the lobster and shrimp at the market."

"Wow, that's impressive," she said. "I should definitely introduce him to Maia someday."

"Your snooty friend Maia?"

"She's not snooty," said Savannah. "She's okay."

"She's not his type. She hates men."

"She doesn't hate men."

"Okay, correction. She hates me," Edward said.

"She's just protective. That's all."

"Okay, whatever," Edward said as he removed his sunglasses from atop his head, pulled his T-shirt off and placed them on the picnic table. He slipped flip-flops from his feet. "Now, while that's cooking, let's go for a swim."

Savannah found herself staring at his arms, chest and abs. Edward had always been in great shape, and the most attractive man she knew. She felt a tingling between her thighs and willed her eyes to look somewhere else.

"Ready?" he asked.

"Not really." Savannah tiptoed across the sand. "There are baby crabs everywhere."

"It's okay, they won't harm you. But just in case..." Edward lifted Savannah into his arms, cradled her and carried her toward the ocean. He picked up his pace and began to run.

"What are you doing?" She laughed and held on to his neck. "Oh my God!"

"Relax." He laughed, too.

"Don't dunk me!" she warned. "I'm not kidding, Edward."

"I'm not going to dunk you." He grinned.

"I mean it! I just got my hair done."

"I'm not going to dunk you."

He placed her gently in the water and she planted her feet just below the surface. She removed her cover-up and tossed it into the sand, walked out into the ocean until the water covered her midsection. Edward rushed into the water with a splash, went for a swim. He crept up behind Savannah and grabbed her. She turned to face him. He picked her up and she wrapped her legs around his waist. She could feel his hardness between her thighs, and it turned her on. She missed him and felt safe in his arms. He held her close and danced about in the water.

They played in the water and laughed. It was natural being with Edward. As if they had never missed a beat—as if divorce had never entered their lives. They stared into each other's eyes.

"Better go check on the food," he whispered.

"Right." She gathered herself and hopped down from his waist.

The two of them headed for the grill, where Edward flipped the seafood with tongs. He pulled a bottle of wine from the cooler and placed it on the table along with two wineglasses. He opened the wine and poured Savannah a glass, handed it to her.

"Here you go, madam," he said. He pulled two disposable plates from the cooler and placed grilled seafood, potatoes and vegetables on each one. "One for you and one for me."

"It smells wonderful."

"I know how much you like seafood. So I cooked all of your favorites."

"Thank you." She blushed.

She took a seat at the table, and Edward sat across from her. They ate and sipped Chardonnay. Edward found soft Caribbean music on his phone.

"So how many women have you brought to this private island and romanced their panties off?"

"What?" Edward laughed and choked on his wine. "This is my first time here."

"You seem to know your way around all too well for it to be your first time."

"It was a carefully thought-out plan to impress you," said Edward. "Is it working?"

She smiled. "I have to admit that I'm quite impressed."

He reached across the table and held on to her hand. "I'm glad."

After dinner, they both cleaned up the mess. The sun began to set and Edward spread two large beach towels on the sand. They sat there facing the ocean. Savannah pulled her knees into her chest and closed her eyes. It was a beautiful night, she thought.

"Thank you for coming to the Bahamas with me. It meant so much for my parents to see Chloe."

"Thank you for inviting us," said Savannah. "This place is gorgeous. This little private island of yours…the one you've never been to before."

"I swear." Edward moved closer. "You're so beautiful."

He reached for her waist, and his lips found hers. She would've pulled away, but she couldn't will her body to move—and her lips defied her. His hand caressed her smooth, silky legs. He lay on his back and then pulled Savannah on top of him. His hands rested against the roundness of her butt. His fingertips found their way beneath the fabric of her bikini bottom, dipped into the sweetness between her thighs. She moaned. His kiss took her breath away. His tongue danced against hers.

He flipped her over onto her back and removed her bottoms. She didn't fight it. Couldn't. He kissed her belly button, then moved down and kissed her inner thigh. His tongue danced inside her, and her toes curled. She remembered the way he'd kissed her there in the past—remembered all too well. His mouth moved upward and nibbled on her breast through the fabric of her bikini top. He loosened the string from around her neck and removed her top, placed her nude breast into his mouth. It sent electricity through her.

He pulled her legs open with his knee and moved his lips back up to her mouth. He removed his trunks with one hand, and when he sprang free, he placed himself inside her. Savannah breathed deeply with the first thrust. She moaned and took in every thrust thereafter. She'd missed him so much. Hadn't found any man who made her feel the way Edward had. Her body shook with desire, and then his. She resisted her urge to cry, couldn't understand why she was so emotional during that moment. He was making her weak again when she'd worked so hard to be strong—to remain in control. She was slowly losing it.

They lay in the sand until they finally saw the lights from *Sophia* in the distance.

"I guess we should get dressed," Edward whispered.

"I guess we should," said Savannah.

She sat up and searched for the pieces of her bikini. She glanced out into the ocean. Didn't want to leave.

Chapter 12

Stephen tied a rope from the cleat of the boat to the dock. Edward climbed out of the boat and then helped Savannah out. He held on to her small hand, a slight grin on his face. He was gaining control of their awkward situation. His goal was to romance her until she no longer wanted to move to London, or at least until she'd agreed to leave Chloe with him. She was playing into his plan. His chest stuck out, his jaws tight. She was just about where he needed her to be.

"It was a pleasure meeting you, Savannah," said Stephen. He gave her a gentle smile. "I can't wait to meet little Chloe. I hear she's adorable."

"It was a pleasure meeting you, too, Stephen. And I'm sure you'll see Chloe before we leave the island."

Stephen hugged and kissed her cheek. He gave Edward a thumbs-up behind her back. Savannah had managed to charm every one of his family members.

"Okay, let's get out of here. Get over to the Grove and pick up Chloe. I'm sure that Jazzy is ready for a break."

"I bet she is, too," Savannah agreed. "Chloe can be a handful."

"I'll see you both at your parents' anniversary party tomorrow night." Stephen gave Edward a strong handshake. "Love you, bro."

"Love you, too," Edward said. "And thank you for today."

"Always." Stephen hopped back into the boat.

Edward and Savannah slid into the backseat of a taxicab, headed for the Grove. He watched her as she stared out the window, reminisced about their afternoon together.

"Are you okay?" he asked.

She gave him a light smile. "Yes."

"Any regrets?"

She shook her head no. "You?"

"None."

As the cab pulled next to the curb, Edward stepped out and walked around to Savannah's side of the car and opened her door. He reached for her hand and she stepped out. He handed the driver a Bahamian bill and the two of them walked into the Grove.

Edward peeked his head into the kitchen. "Hello, Raquel," he greeted the Grove's cook.

"Hello, bebby. How are you?" she asked in her Bahamian accent.

"I'm great. Have you seen my sister Jasmine and her little sidekick?"

"Oh, you mean Miss Chloe?" She giggled. "The two of them left about an hour ago. Jazzy said she was headed home to Governor's Harbour."

"To my parents'?"

"Yes."

"Okay, thanks, Raquel."

"Can I fix you and the missus some supper?" she asked.

"That would be nice. Maybe something light. Thank you."

"I think there's some conch salad in the fridge. Can I fix you some?"

"That sounds wonderful," said Edward as he pulled his cell phone out to call Jasmine.

He stepped away from the kitchen.

"Yes, Edward," Jasmine answered on the second ring.

"What's up?" he asked.

"We're on Governor's Harbour," Jasmine said.

"Are you coming back, or do you want us to come there and pick up Chloe?"

"Leave her. She's in pajamas and watching movies with her uncle Nate. She would be disappointed if she had to leave now."

"May I speak with her?"

"Of course," she said, and then yelled Chloe's name in his ear. "Here she comes."

"You couldn't hold the phone away instead of yelling in my ear?" Edward asked.

"Sorry." Jasmine giggled. "Did you have a good time with Savannah today?"

"It was okay," he tried to appear nonchalant about the evening.

"Do I hear wedding bells?" Jasmine asked.

"What? No!"

"Are you telling me that it's completely out of the question?"

He looked at Savannah, who was hanging on his every word. "I'm telling you that I'd like to speak with my daughter, please."

"Here, sweetheart. It's your daddy," he heard Jasmine say.

"Hi, Daddy." Chloe's voice was music to Edward's ears.

"Hello, sweetheart. What are you doing?"

"I'm watching a movie with Uncle Nate," she explained. "Can I spend the night? Grandpa promised me hot chocolate and pancakes in the morning."

"Wow. Hot chocolate *and* pancakes? Who could say no to that? Let me just see if it's okay with Mommy." Edward gave Savannah a glance. She nodded a yes. "Mommy says it's okay."

"Yay!" Chloe exclaimed.

"Now, let me warn you… Grandpa's pancakes probably aren't as good as Daddy's…"

"Stop it." Savannah laughed.

"…but you should still be polite and eat them all up," Edward continued. "And tell him how good they are."

Chloe giggled. "Okay, Daddy."

"Mommy and I will see you in the morning."

"Okay, Daddy. I love you."

"I love you more," Edward said.

"Tell her I love her, too," Savannah whispered.

"Mommy loves you, too," Edward said.

"Love you, Mommy!" Chloe exclaimed. "Daddy, can you give her a kiss for me?"

"I certainly will." He glanced over at Savannah and winked.

He'd give her a kiss, but not the kind that Chloe referred to. His kiss would mean something different. He became aroused at the thought of it. As much as he wanted to believe that the afternoon had been about convincing her to change her mind about taking Chloe to London, he knew there was much more going on in his heart than he was willing to admit.

They feasted on conch salad and conch fritters while relaxing in the cabana. Edward leaned back in his chair and took in the light Bahamian breeze. He sipped on a Bahamian beer, while Savannah drank her second sky juice.

"That's my mother's favorite drink, you know. Sky juice," Edward stated. "She drinks them more often than I'd like her to."

"I can see why. They're delicious," said Savannah. "Never had one before."

"Careful. They sneak up on you," Edward said.

"Wouldn't you love for that to happen?" Savannah flirted.

"Do you think that I took advantage of you on the beach?"

"Didn't you?"

"I thought we were two consenting adults, enjoying each other."

"It was very emotional for me," Savannah admitted. "It's been a long time since we…you know…have been together. The setting was perfect and it was just so damn romantic!"

"So had there been a less romantic setting…"

"I think it was inevitable, no matter the setting." He knew that she was becoming inebriated. "I was drawn to you from the beginning."

"From the beginning of what?" Edward laughed. He knew that he shouldn't discuss these things with her while under the influence, but he found satisfaction in knowing her true feelings.

"Since the beginning of time, silly. I've loved you and wanted you since the moment I met you. That never changed."

Edward was startled by her announcement.

"You divorced me!" he stated.

"Because you didn't have time for us—me or our daughter. And because of Quinn."

"She's never been more than a friend, Savannah. I swear to you."

"You said that," she proclaimed. "I just never felt like Chloe and I were your priority."

They were flirting with danger by discussing such a painful time. The Bahamas was not the place for old wounds, and this was not the time. He wasn't willing to move backward after he'd made such strides.

"Maybe we should go upstairs, and I'll run you a hot bath."

"Maybe we should," Savannah agreed.

She stood and stumbled. Edward rushed to her side, grabbed her, and escorted her back inside and up to her room. He gently placed her on the bed. He went into the bathroom and started the water in the bathtub. When he came back into the room she was struggling to remove her shoes. Finally kicked them to the floor.

"You okay?" he asked.

"I'm fine." She laughed and then curled into a fetal position.

"I'm running you a hot bath. Do you have some bubbles or some smell-good stuff somewhere?"

She pointed across the room, at her bag.

He unzipped the outer pocket in search of her bath products. No luck. He looked inside, and came upon her cell phone. She'd forgotten to turn it off. He'd warned her that international rates would be astronomical. He grabbed her phone to turn it off and noticed a text message from a Florida exchange.

I can definitely get a passport for your daughter. We don't need her father's consent. Call my office when you return to the States and we'll discuss it. Enjoy the Bahamas!

He tossed the phone back into the bag. He was livid. He glanced over at Savannah as light snores escaped from her mouth. She was soundly sleeping, but he wanted to shake her. He took a seat in the Georgian-style wing chair in the corner of the room, watched her as she slept. His mind raced as he tried to decide how he would confront her. He needed an explanation. Did she really think that she could go behind his back and get Chloe a passport without his consent? She had a lot of nerve.

He went into the bathroom and shut off the running water. He left the room and decided he needed to go for a walk. He went through the lobby and past the kitchen.

"Can I get you and the missus anything else tonight, Mr. Talbot?" asked Raquel.

"No thanks, Raquel. She's sleeping."

"You need some hot tea?"

"Something stronger."

"It's that bad?" Raquel gave him a knowing grin. "Drinking is only a temporary fix for things."

"It's all I need," he stated and then headed for the cabana. "Good night, Raquel."

"Good night, bebby."

He stopped at the bar and asked for a vodka and grapefruit juice. The bartender slid the glass in front of him and he paid with a Bahamian bill.

"Keep the change, Deuce," he told the Rastafarian bartender.

"Thank you, sir." Deuce slipped the extra bills into the tip jar on the bar.

Edward headed toward the darkness of the beach. He plopped down into a chair and sipped on vodka. He found a relaxing Caribbean playlist on his phone and leaned his head back. Fell asleep while listening.

* * *

"What are you doing out here?" Jasmine was standing over him.

The sun stood in the corner of the sky and beamed down on his face as he struggled to open his eyes.

"What time is it?" he asked, realizing he'd been there all night.

"Seven thirty."

"You're here early," he stated as he straightened in the chair.

"Your daughter's an early riser, dude. Little girl was up at the crack of dawn having pancakes and chocolate milk with your father."

A smile crept into the side of Edward's mouth. "Where is she now?"

"She's inside with Savannah," said Jasmine. "Did you two have a fight?"

"No. Why do you ask?"

"Because she didn't know where the hell you were, and then I find you out here asleep on the beach!"

"She got a little tipsy last night. Passed out. So I came out here to clear my head."

"And you're okay?"

"I'm fine." He stood, grabbed his empty glass, wrapped his arm around his sister's shoulder.

"Whatever's going on, you can talk to me about it," she said. "I'll listen and only offer advice if you ask for it."

He decided that he needed an ally. A confidant. "She's trying to take Chloe away from me. She's moving to London to be with her mother, and taking Chloe with her."

"Seriously?" Jasmine gave Edward a puzzled look. "Can she do that?"

"She's taking me to court to petition for it."

"Then what are you two doing here together? I'm confused."

"I wanted Chloe to see all of you, and thought it was the perfect time with everyone being home," he said. "And I brought her along to try to convince her not to go, or to leave Chloe with me. I can't live without my daughter, Jazzy."

"She's the air you breathe. I know that. Everyone knows that."

"It doesn't matter. Her mind's made up."

"I know Savannah. She's a good person. She loves you, and she knows that you love Chloe. She'll do what's right."

He needed Jasmine's optimism, though he wasn't convinced that things were that simple. He wasn't sure that Savannah would surely do what was right. If she was able to get a passport for Chloe without his consent, she could probably get her out of the country without his knowledge as well.

Chapter 13

The Grand Room was decorated in royal blue and silver. White lilies adorned the room. It reminded Savannah of her wedding day. She'd insisted on bouquets of calla lilies for her bridal attendants. Her favorite flower was expensive, but Edward had promised that she could have whatever her heart desired.

Edward had been a handsome groom, wearing a black tuxedo with a silky gray vest and gray tie to match. He was young back then. They both were. But they'd matured over the years. This weekend, they'd found each other again. At least Savannah thought they had. She wasn't sure which direction their relationship would go once they returned to Florida, but she knew that it wasn't the same as it had been before coming to the Bahamas.

She watched as Edward held a glass of champagne in the air, offered a toast to his parents on their anniversary. He was their oldest child. Beverly Talbot had been pregnant with him before the couple married. They had a beautiful love story and Savannah loved listening to it, especially when Beverly Talbot told it.

Edward's father, Paul John, had attended Howard University in Washington, DC, where he met her. She was a young student, and they hit it off right away. While Beverly studied to become a teacher, Paul John studied medicine—and in between studying, the two fell in love. After graduating from medical school, Paul John applied for residency at a hospital in Key West, and landed the opportunity with flying colors. However, this opportunity posed a problem for his new girlfriend. Beverly, who'd always called the District of Columbia her home, was offered a position to teach at a prestigious school in Maryland. It appeared that this was the end of their four-year love affair. It seemed logical that they pursue their own separate careers—after all, opportunities didn't fall out of the sky, and there were no guarantees that they'd receive them again. Neither of the two wanted to hinder the other's progress.

Confident that he'd made the most practical decision, Paul John took a train back to Key West, leaving Beverly behind. He managed to bury himself in his work during the first several months of his residency, yet his heart still longed for her. When she showed up in the emergency room of his hospital, bags in tow and with a swollen belly, he was happier than any man could be. His life changed completely that night, and the anticipation of marriage and fatherhood had him on top of the world.

It appeared to Savannah that he remained on top of the world, even until this day—their thirty-seventh wedding anniversary. Savannah wished that she and Edward could've had such a story. She wished their marriage had withstood the test of time, and that they could proudly stand before Chloe one day and celebrate their thirty-seventh wedding anniversary. But things hadn't turned out quite the way they'd anticipated. In fact, their union hadn't even lasted two years. And for that, Savannah felt ashamed. She tried not to focus on her and Edward's discrepancies, but instead glanced over at the beautiful lady of the hour.

Beverly Talbot looked stunning in her silver gown, her hair in a perfect bun atop her head. Her makeup was flawless. She'd sacrificed so much for her family, and Savannah admired her former mother-in-law. She'd been the strong woman in Savannah's life after her own mother had abandoned her. Beverly Talbot had been the voice of reason on the other end of the phone many days before and after she and Edward divorced. Savannah loved her.

Tears welled in her eyes as she listened to Edward and his siblings speak with such admiration and respect for their parents. She only wished that her and Edward's love had been long-standing. Suddenly it occurred to her that they'd given up much too easily. When things got tough, she ran to her father's home. She wondered what would've been had she stayed and made it work.

A Caribbean version of Etta James's "At Last" began to play. Paul John grabbed Beverly's waist and moved her toward the dance floor. He drew her close and began to dance slowly to the music. Jackson grabbed Jasmine by the hand, and the two held each other close. Samson spun Alyson and then wrapped his strong arm around her shoulder. The couples moved to the music. Edward glanced at her from across the room. He hadn't rushed to her side as she'd expected him to. In fact, he'd been standoffish for most of the day.

He finally made his way over to her. "Care to dance?" he asked.

"Sure," said Savannah as she took his hand. She turned to Chloe, who was seated at a table. "We'll be right back, baby."

As they danced close, she breathed in his scent, and thoughts of their lovemaking rushed through her mind.

He looked down into her eyes, and she stared into his. He wore a sensible blue tuxedo, and his goatee was perfectly trimmed. The smell of his cologne danced against her nose.

"I thought you'd never ask," she told him.

"You look beautiful," he whispered.

She'd found the charcoal-gray after-five gown at a local bridal boutique in Palm Beach. It was a must-have and the price tag had caught her eye, marked down by 70 percent. The back revealed bare skin, and the split up the side unveiled long, sexy legs. Edward grabbed the small of her back, and she rested her face against his neck.

"Thank you. You look very handsome."

He smiled. "I do my best."

"It's our last night here in the Bahamas. What are we doing tonight?"

"I think I'm going to spend the night in Governor's Harbour, at my parents' house," he said. "Need to spend some time with everyone before we all part ways. No telling when I'll see them all again."

"That sounds great. Do you think there's room for Chloe and me?"

"Um...yeah..." He was hesitant, and that caught her off guard. "I think there's room."

"You sure?" she asked.

"Yeah, I think there's room."

"Good! Then we'll come, too," she exclaimed.

She loved the Talbots and couldn't wait to spend another evening with all of them.

"Pardon me, big brother." Edward's younger brother Nate approached. "Can I cut in?"

"No, you can't cut in!" Edward teased.

"Why not?" Nate asked. "You afraid she might think I'm a better dancer, or much better-looking?"

"Neither of the two."

"Then step aside, chump." He pushed Edward aside and grabbed Savannah by the waist. "I need a dance with this beautiful lady while the night is still young."

"Hello, Nate." Savannah kissed his cheek. "So good to see you."

"You, too! You're looking beautiful as always," he said. "I didn't believe them when they told me you were here on the island! And with Edward."

Edward lifted his hands in surrender and exited the dance floor.

"He invited Chloe and me for the weekend…for your parents' anniversary party. I'm so happy for them."

"Yeah, me, too. They have plenty of years in. That's a long time to be with one person."

"When are you going to find that special woman to spend your life with?"

"I don't know if she's out there, sis. I've had too much pain."

"Of course she's out there! You just have to look for her."

"What about you? You doing okay?"

"I am."

"You and my brother getting back together?"

"I… We're just really good friends," Savannah stated. In her heart she felt that she and Edward might be moving toward something more than friendship, but she didn't want to be presumptuous.

"I want you both to be happy. So whatever that means, I'm down for that."

"Thanks, Nate."

She had grown fond of Edward's brother Nate over the years. He'd come to live with them briefly one summer during his college days. He thought he wanted a career in politics and decided to shadow his brother. He quickly became bored with following Edward around town, and headed back to Atlanta to what he considered a much more exciting life.

There were a number of lonely nights he'd kept Savannah in good company with games of Scrabble and watching multiple episodes of *Family Feud.* He'd resented his brother for making more time for his career, and not enough for his wife and newborn child—thought that Edward was a fool for squandering his marriage. He'd have given anything to have a woman like Savannah in his corner.

"You'll always be my sister-in-law, no matter what," Nate said. "My brother's a fool if he doesn't get you back in his life. And I'll tell him that to his face."

Denny tapped Nate on the shoulder. "My turn, bro."

"I'm still dancing," Nate protested. "Go dance with Jazzy or Alyson."

"I don't want to dance with them. I want to dance with Savannah."

"Where's your little GI Jane?"

"She went back to the US. She got all pissed off about Sage."

"Well, what did you expect? A parade?" Nate asked, and then continued to dance with Savannah. "You have a lot to learn about women."

"This from someone who doesn't have a woman." Denny grabbed Savannah by the hand.

Nate sighed, and then worked his way outside to the cabana, where Edward had gone just moments before. After dancing with Denny, Savannah made her way back to the table where Chloe waited patiently.

"Hey, baby, are you okay?"

"Yes, Mommy," said Chloe.

"Hey, Savannah." Edward's sister Whitney approached. Whitney wore her natural hair in an up-style. She wore a short evening gown that boasted her curvy figure and long lean legs. Her brown skin was like her mother's, and her smile lit up the darkest of rooms. Though she was an elementary school teacher, she looked nothing like the stereotype. "How are you?"

"Whitney!" Savannah exclaimed. "Great seeing you."

"You, too. They told me you were here." Whitney smiled. "You look good."

"So do you."

"My flight just arrived about an hour ago. So I am exhausted! Jet lag is a beast," Whitney said. "Is this Chloe?"

"Yes."

"Hello, beautiful," she said to Chloe.

"Hello."

"Isn't she gorgeous?" Jasmine asked as she walked up. "Come on, sweetie. Let's go get punch and cake. Lots of sugar!"

"This is what she does," said Whitney. "She fills your children up with sugar and then sends them home with you. I can't wait until she has kids of her own."

"Well, you might not have to wait long for that." Jasmine gently touched her stomach.

Whitney stared at her sister with an open mouth. "What are you saying, Jasmine Talbot?"

"Yeah, what *are* you saying?" Savannah asked.

"Well..." She smiled shyly. "I don't know for sure, but I'm late."

"What?"

"I have an appointment on Monday. And I'll know for sure then."

Whitney grabbed her sister in a strong embrace. "I'm so excited."

Savannah glanced across the room at Jasmine's husband,

Jackson. He looked at the trio speculatively. Wondered what the excitement was about.

"Shh. Jackson doesn't know yet. Nobody knows, except for you two. And I want to keep it that way until I know for sure."

"My lips are sealed," said Whitney.

They both looked at Savannah.

"Mine, too."

"No revealing anything to Edward," Jasmine warned.

Savannah made the motion of zipping her lips. "Mum's the word."

"Where is my big brother anyway?" Whitney asked.

"I think I saw him at the bar," said Jasmine. "Chloe and I are going for cake and punch. Chloe, my lady."

Chloe hopped up from her chair, locked arms with Jasmine and followed her across the room.

"I should go say hello to my parents first," Whitney said. She gave Savannah a hug. "It was great seeing you."

"You, too."

Savannah made her way out to the cabana bar to find Edward. Stood next to him. "Care if I join you?" she asked.

He motioned for her to take a seat next to his. "Where's Chloe?"

"With Jazzy, of course."

"Those two are joined at the hip. They've grown quite fond of each other. Can't wait until Jazzy has kids of her own." He chuckled.

Savannah laughed at the thought, too.

"What are you drinking?" Edward asked.

"Sky juice."

Edward gave her a sideways look. "Sky juice, huh?"

"It's grown on me."

"You and my mother," said Edward. "Deuce, give the lady a sky juice."

Deuce nodded, and Savannah followed Edward's gaze to the mounted television.

"Soccer." she smiled.

She fondly remembered Edward insisting that their local cable company carry the Bahamian channels so that he could watch soccer on the weekends. They never did, and he never recovered.

"I have to come to the Bahamas to see it."

"I remember the letter that you wrote to the corporate offices of Time Warner that year."

"I wanted them to know that I was serious!" Edward laughed. "American men have Monday Night Football. There are more Bahamian men in Florida than people realize. Why couldn't we have a soccer channel?"

"You're great at fighting for causes. You should've taken it further."

"It was a lost cause." He sipped on his Bahamian beer. "Just like a lot of other causes that I fight for."

She felt there was an underlying message in his statement, but she chose to ignore it. Deuce slid the glass of gin with coconut water in front of her, and she took a long sip.

"Mmm. That's good," she said.

"Edward Talbot!" The voice was loud. Whitney shook her hips as she headed their way. "Hey, big brother."

Edward smiled and shook his head. "Can you be any louder?"

"Are you hungover?" Whitney smiled.

"No, I'm not hungover." Edward stood and gave his sister a strong hug.

"I see that you and Savannah are hanging out again. What does that mean?" She sang the last few words.

"It means that she's here…enjoying the Bahamas. And our parents' anniversary party."

"With you." Whitney smiled. "Are we reconciling?"

"No." Savannah and Edward said it at the same time.

"Okay. We'll see," said Whitney. "My brother's a good man, Savannah. You should give him a second chance. And just so you know, Edward hasn't brought any other woman here to the Bahamas…since you two…you, know. Split. I don't think he's even had any…"

"Enough!" Edward exclaimed.

Savannah and Whitney giggled.

"Okay, I'm leaving," said Whitney. "But you think about what I said, Savannah Talbot. Is your name still Talbot? Or did you go back to your maiden name?"

"Goodbye, Whitney," said Edward.

"I'm leaving." Whitney laughed. "But I need a drink first. Deuce, give me a glass of Merlot, please. And put it on my brother's tab."

Deuce nodded and poured Whitney a glass of wine. She grabbed it and bid the couple a good night, walked back inside.

"I'm ready to head over to Governor's Harbour," Edward said. "Do you need to pack a bag or something for you and Chloe?"

"Yes, I'll go up and do that now." Savannah slid from her bar stool. She grabbed her drink. "I'll be back shortly."

"I'll be right here waiting."

She sashayed toward the Grand Room, hoped that Edward was watching her walk away. She turned around to see. He was.

Chapter 14

Edward decided that he wouldn't spend the last night of his trip stewing over the text message he had run across on Savannah's phone. He'd let it go, just for the night. He'd address it with her the moment they were back in Florida, though. But for the night, he would enjoy his family.

George Symonette's voice filled the house, along with the smell of johnnycakes and fresh seafood. Bottles of wine were lined up on the coffee table, and Edward's mother and father danced in the middle of the floor. Edward removed his Calvin Klein loafers from his feet and leaned back on the sofa. Chloe hopped onto his lap. He sipped on a Bahamian beer and watched as his family enjoyed their time together.

"Where's Samson and his guitar?" Beverly Talbot asked. "I want him to play something."

"Yes, that would be great," said Jackson.

"Jackson should sing," Edward insisted.

"Alyson, go tell your hubby that Mom wants a selection," said Whitney.

"Go tell him yourself." Alyson waved her hand in the air and leaned back in her father's easy chair. "He's out on the front porch sulking. We had a fight in the cab on the way over."

Whitney huffed and headed for the porch. "I don't know how he puts up with you."

"I don't know how I put up with him." Alyson tossed her hair. "And I don't know where he's sleeping tonight, because he's certainly not sleeping with me."

"Sweetheart, he has to sleep with you. We're limited on space. And since Edward and Savannah can't sleep together, we need all the room we can get." Beverly Talbot smiled at Savannah and Edward. "Sorry, babies, but we're Baptists, and you're not married anymore, and we can't have you sleeping in the same bed. Now, if you decide to remarry…"

"Mother, it's okay," Edward interjected as every eye in the house landed on him. "We're good."

Savannah smiled sweetly, embarrassment written on her face.

They were both relieved when Samson came into the house with his guitar.

"What would you like to hear, Mother?" he asked.

"Oh, I don't know. Something sweet. A love song," said Beverly.

"Something a little more contemporary than George Symonette," Nate suggested. "No offense, Mother and Pop."

"None taken," said Paul John.

Beverly rolled her eyes at her son. "Fine. Something a little more contemporary."

"Something by Beres Hammond," Jasmine suggested.

"These American boys don't know anything about Beres," Nate teased.

Jackson turned to Samson. "Let's show them what these American boys do know."

Samson sat on the edge of the sofa. His acoustic guitar rested on his leg, and his fingertips began to fret the strings. He began to play the tune of Beres Hammond's "I Feel Good." Jackson started to sing the lyrics. Samson closed his eyes. He didn't see that Alyson's demeanor had changed, and she was hanging on to every word of the song. When he opened his eyes, he smiled at her. Edward bobbed his head and looked over at Savannah, who was consumed by the lyrics as well. He gave her a warm smile.

The duo began to play "Stranger in Town."

"Isn't that your song, Edward?" Nate asked. "Yours and Savannah's?"

"Yes! Get up, you two, and dance!" Whitney insisted.

"Not right now," said Edward.

"As good a time as any," Jasmine said.

"Oh, come on." Beverly Talbot grabbed Chloe in her arms and pulled her son up from the sofa.

Edward and Savannah began to dance. She moved her hips to the music.

"She moves like she's Bahamian!" Jasmine said. "Work those hips, girl."

Jasmine and Denny danced together, and Whitney pulled Alyson up from her chair and the pair danced. Alyson's bad attitude slowly dissipated as the music resonated through her body. She smiled at her husband as he played his guitar and as Jackson sang the lyrics of the Bahamian love song.

It was these times that Edward loved and missed most about home. Times like this gave him life—wrongs were righted during these visits home. He gave Savannah a slow spin and then pulled her close. He looked into her eyes and wanted to kiss her lips at that moment. Had to remember where he was. He didn't realize that the entire family was watching him as he watched her.

* * *

After the women were settled in their beds, the men sat on the front porch, a bottle of Bahamian beer in each one's hand as they told lies and laughed about the good things and complained about the bad. Caribbean music played lightly on an old radio. The moon was brightly situated in the corner of the dark sky, stars played hide-and-seek, and the smell of the ocean swept along with the wind every time it decided to blow.

"Sir, you and Mrs. Talbot have been married for longer than I've been on this earth," said Samson. "How did you do it?"

"Forget it," Nate said. "You're married to Alyson. There's no hope for you, boy."

Laughter filled the porch.

"It's not easy, son, but there is hope," Paul John said. "You put up with things that you don't always want to put up with. You love them when they're unlovable. You smile when you're hurting inside. You agree when you don't want to. You make it work."

"And you don't bail when things get tough," Nate said, and then glanced at Edward.

"Are you speaking to me?" Edward asked.

"Just in general," Nate said. "When you have a good woman, you don't bail on her."

"Why don't you just say it, Nate? Whatever it is that you need to say. Obviously you have something you need to get off your chest," said Edward.

"I was speaking in general, but since you brought it up, I think you squandered your relationship with Savannah."

"For your information, she divorced me. She ran off to Georgia to her father's house and didn't come back!"

"She ran off because you weren't showing her any attention. You were too occupied with your career and that damn campaign manager of yours. What was her name? Quinn?"

"I'm sorry. How is this any of your business?"

"It's not."

"Good. Then let it go."

Nate waved his beer in the air. "It's gone. But if I were you, I wouldn't let her get away a second time. She clearly still loves your ass. I can't imagine why, but she does."

"You were letting it go, remember?" asked Edward.

Nate waved his bottle of beer in the air again. "Gone."

"And what makes you think she still loves me anyway?" Edward pushed. "Did she say something to you?"

"She didn't have to. The world can see that you both still love each other." Nate stood. "Anybody want another beer?"

"I'm good," Jackson said.

"Bring me one," said Samson.

"None for me," Denny said. "I have an early flight."

"You, Pop?" Nate asked.

"No, son, I'm done for the night," said Paul John.

"Edward?"

"What is it with you and Savannah, anyway? Do you want her?" Edward stood. "You've always had this little thing for her. This little crush. So let's just get it out there in the open. Would you like a roll in the hay with my ex-wife, Nathan Talbot?"

"What are you talking about?"

"I'm talking about this little obsession you've always had for her."

"Pop, get your son. Please tell him to sit back down before I have to drop him."

"Nobody's dropping anybody," said Paul John.

"Don't talk to Pop as if I'm not standing here. Talk to me. I'm right here."

"To answer your question, no, I'm not interested in Savannah or any other woman. As a matter of fact, I'm not interested in women at all, big brother. And it's been that way for some time. So you have nothing to worry about."

A disturbed Edward sat back down. "What?"

"There. It's out there. Nobody has to speculate anymore. It's right out there in the open," Nate said.

Every man on the porch was left speechless as Nate went inside. Slammed the screen door behind him.

"I know he's not saying what I think he's saying," Edward said. "What do you do with that information, Pop? How do you deal with that? Aren't you going to demand that he come back and explain himself?"

"He's my son, and I love him. That's how I deal with it," said Paul John.

"That doesn't disturb you one bit? He always gets away with stuff. Always has."

"I don't necessarily agree with any of your lifestyles. You or your siblings, but I love each of you, in spite of yourselves. Individually. Nothing can change that."

Edward reclined in his seat. Took a long sip of his beer. Paul John Talbot didn't get excited about much, Edward knew that, but he wanted his father to get excited this time—to chastise Nate for once. They were Baptists, as his mother was always so quick to remind him. Yet Nate's revelation had gone unchallenged.

"There was some truth about what he said about you, though. It's clear that you still love Savannah and that she still loves you. What will you do with that, son? That's the question." Paul John stood and then walked into the house.

Chapter 15

Edward's head bounced against the leather seat. He fought sleep and wanted to be awake to think things through. He needed a plan, and he needed to come up with it long before the wheels of the jet hit the runway. He had to know which direction he was going to take this relationship with Savannah. His plan for romance in the Bahamas had been successful. But he wasn't sure if he'd romanced her enough to keep her from leaving the country.

When he married Savannah, his mother had insisted that he give her the family ring—the vintage ring with the oval emerald in the center. Tiny diamonds danced around the outer edge of the center stone. It was the ring that his grandfather, Clyde Talbot, had given his bride when they wed. His grandmother had worn it until her death.

"You're Clyde Talbot's oldest grandchild," his mother had told him. "Your father and I want you to give it to Savannah when you propose."

"Are you sure? It's an expensive ring, and a family heirloom. That's a lot of pressure."

"Your grandfather would want you to have it," Beverly had insisted.

He'd taken the ring. And when he'd proposed to Savannah, he explained the significance of it. Her tears were an indication that she understood. She had been honored to wear his grandmother's ring and promised never to take it for granted. She would live up to its legacy, she swore. And she had.

After the divorce, she'd returned it. Placed it in his hand right there at the courthouse. "Thank you for letting me borrow this," she'd said.

He had returned the ring to his mother, hoped that one of his other brothers would have better luck in love. However, during this visit, he'd built up the nerve to ask for it back.

"You're going to ask her again?" his mother had asked. "I knew."

"I should never have left," he'd told his mother.

"You're right." She'd placed her hand against his face. "I told you that."

"I'm not made of the same stuff my father is made of, Mother. He's much stronger than I am. Braver."

"He's no stronger or braver."

"I failed her. And my daughter. And I need to make it right."

His mother placed the emerald in his hand and then closed his fingers around it. "I don't want this ring back, Edward Talbot. Not unless I outlive Savannah. Which I pray doesn't happen."

"I hear you, Mother."

"Don't go back for the wrong reasons, either. Go back because you love her, and only that. And if you love her, then Edward, give it everything you have to make it work this time."

"I will."

* * *

He glanced over at Savannah as the plane soared to new heights. Her head rested against the window and light snores crept from her lips. He stared for a moment. Wondered what her dreams were made of. When the time was right, he was going to ask her to be his wife again. He was ready to start anew, give their family a chance. He could see himself loving Savannah again. They'd connected in the Bahamas, and his family already loved her to death. Her father might not be so welcoming, but he would deal with him. Edward would respect the man regardless.

He'd even forgiven Savannah for attempting to get a passport for Chloe under false pretenses and without his consent. He'd also forgiven her for filing the petition for relocation and having him served at his downtown office. None of it would matter once they were married.

He pulled into the driveway of the home that used to be his and turned off the engine. He got out, reached for a sleeping Chloe and pulled her out of the backseat, then followed Savannah to the door as she unlocked it. He took Chloe to her room and placed her in bed. He tramped back down the hardwood staircase and then unloaded their luggage from the trunk, placed it next to the stairwell.

"You need me to take it upstairs?" he asked.

"No, I think I can manage from here," said Savannah. "Thank you for a lovely weekend."

"Thank you for coming along."

"Chloe and I both had a wonderful time with your family," she said. "And the beach. I particularly enjoyed the private island and the beach."

"Hmm. I'm glad." He smiled. "Let's get together this week. I'd like to take you out to dinner, talk about some things. You think you can get a sitter for Chloe…maybe Friday?"

"Yeah, I think so."

"Good." He kissed her cheek and then gently kissed her lips. He held on to her hand. "I'll give you a call later."

"Okay."

Their hands lingered together for a moment. He looked at her ring finger, caressed it. It looked like it needed a little bling. The beautiful stone would look good there, just as it had before. He let her go and almost skipped to his car. He'd give it a week. Be sure he was making the right decision. With all things considered, he would be an engaged man by Friday night.

Edward hit his garage door opener as he pulled into his subdivision. The first thing he noticed was the red Mercedes with the top dropped, parked in front of his house. Quinn stepped out when she saw him pull into the driveway.

"I just took a chance and picked up your favorite!" She held a white plastic bag in the air. "Thai."

"How did you know what time I'd be here?"

"I just said I took a chance." She giggled. "I got Thai basil shrimp, spicy curry chicken, green curry tofu for the weird guy who prefers to not eat meat."

"The weird guy, huh?"

He decided to leave his bags in the trunk. He'd grab them later. Instead he walked in through the garage with Quinn close on his heels. She wasn't hesitant about going straight to his kitchen. She pulled two plates from the shelf and grabbed two forks and two wineglasses.

"Don't be shy. Make yourself at home," he said sarcastically.

"Don't mind if I do." Quinn prepared a plate of green curry tofu for Edward. "So how was the trip?"

"Nice."

"Your parents' anniversary party was spectacular?"

"Wonderful," said Edward, "and it was great seeing my family. All my sisters and brothers were there. I took Chloe *and* Savannah, too."

"Really? I didn't know that Savannah went." Quinn's demeanor changed a bit. "Something I need to know?"

"No."

"Wow, you took her to the Bahamas. That's different," Quinn said as she made herself a plate. She walked over to Edward's wine rack, grabbed a bottle of Chardonnay. "Where's the corkscrew?"

"Top drawer." Edward sat at the island in the kitchen, a plate of Thai food in front of him. He grabbed a fork and dug in. "This is good."

"I know it is. The best damn Thai food in Florida." She found the corkscrew and opened the bottle of wine. Poured two glasses.

"I'm thinking about asking Savannah to marry me again," he stated.

"Yeah?" She pretended not to be alarmed by the news. "What makes you think she wants to remarry your behind?"

"Because I'm a good man. And I'm her baby's daddy—" he rubbed his chin "—and I'm fine as hell."

"You are all of those things," she said, "but that doesn't necessarily warrant a marriage proposal, Casanova."

"No, it doesn't. But love does. I realized that I still love her, and I think we can make this work." He pulled the emerald out of the pocket of his shirt and showed Quinn. "My mother gave me the ring back, and I'm going to propose."

"Wow! That's, uh…" She cleared her throat, took a drink of her wine. "That's deep. A lot must've happened on that trip."

"A lot did." Edward finished the helping of food and

took a gulp of wine. "I'm going up and hop in the shower. I'm really tired and want to just unwind."

"Sure, I will—I'll just finish up here and clean up my mess," said Quinn. "I'll let myself out."

"You sure?" he asked.

"Of course. No worries. Go take a shower."

"Okay, cool. Maybe I'll see you at the office tomorrow," Edward said as he headed to his bedroom. "Or maybe I won't."

"You will! Because you're a workaholic!"

"I'll be there," he replied.

He knew that Quinn would be bothered by his news about Savannah, which was why he gave it to her straight, no chaser. She needed to know sooner rather than later. Plus he needed to hear himself say it to her. Somehow that made it real. In addition, he knew that it was necessary for their friendship to change if he had any hopes of a future with Savannah. He would slowly disconnect from her. She would chafe at it, but he had to do it. He couldn't risk losing Savannah again. He had to fight for them with all of his might this time.

Chapter 16

The moment Savannah lifted the black suitcase to carry it upstairs, she knew that it wasn't hers. It was too heavy. Edward had gotten their luggage mixed up again. She had his suitcase, and he had hers. They'd had matching luggage for years, and she'd sworn that she was going to buy something brighter in color, not the drab black leather bag that she'd owned for too long. She needed her bag—her toiletries, makeup and other unmentionables were inside. She called his cell phone. It went straight to his voice mail.

"Shoot," she whispered.

She slipped a pair of sandals onto her feet and loaded a sleepy Chloe into the backseat of her car.

"We have to go see Daddy," she explained to her five-year-old. "He took the wrong luggage. I promise we'll be back soon, and you can get back into your comfy bed. Are you hungry?"

"Yes," said Chloe.

"Maybe we'll grab a pizza on the way back."

"With pepperoni?"

"Whatever you want, sweetie. Now buckle up."

Savannah drove across town to Edward's neighborhood. She hoped he would answer his phone—save her the trouble of unloading Chloe and coming inside. He could just bring the luggage out to the car, and make the switch without her having to lift a finger. She was drained, and wanted nothing more than a long, hot shower and to hop into a pair of sweats and a T-shirt. She had a long day ahead of her. It was time to pack up her office and prepare for her future. She'd decided to put London on hold for a bit, at least until she determined what it was that she and Edward were doing. She felt as if they'd reconnected, bonded, and perhaps they had a chance at a real future. She owed it to herself and Chloe to at least find out.

She pulled up in front of his house and noticed the red Mercedes parked out front. He had company. She dialed his number again. It rang this time.

"Hello," said the female voice on the other end.

"I'm sorry, I must have the wrong number."

"Who are you looking for?"

"Edward Talbot."

"You have the right number."

Her hands shook, and her heart beat rapidly. "May I ask who this is?"

"It's Quinn."

She'd suspected that it was. "Is Edward available? He mixed up our luggage again, and I just need to get my bag."

"He's showering right now," she said. "We were about to turn in for the night. Can I give him a message?"

She was enjoying this. Savannah could hear the satisfaction in her voice.

"No. None." She quickly hung up. Sat there for a moment to gather her emotions.

She hated him at that moment. They'd been in town for less than a few hours and Quinn was already in his home, and obviously in his bed, too. Tears threatened to fall from her eyes, but she willed them not to. She wouldn't cry over Edward again. She had no more tears for him. She couldn't for the life of her figure out why he would drag her all the way to the Bahamas, seduce her and then break her heart again. And she didn't want to know. She just wanted to forget that Edward Talbot existed.

She pulled into her driveway and sat there for a moment, a pepperoni pizza in the passenger seat next to her and Chloe asleep in the backseat. Those tears that she'd willed not to fall earlier were much stronger than she thought. They had a mind of their own, and slowly crept down the side of her face and burned her cheeks. She turned her head and looked out the window. Here she was feeling this way again. She pulled her cell phone out again. Pulled up the text message from Maia's friend at the State Department. Responded.

Change of heart. I will need that passport for my daughter after all.
ASAP! When can we meet?

She wiped tears from her eyes, got herself together and then stepped out of the car. She reached into the backseat of the car.

"Let's go inside, baby," she said to Chloe and lifted her out of her car seat. "Mommy's got pizza."

After eating and putting Chloe to bed, she cleaned the kitchen. Her cell phone buzzed and she looked at the screen. Edward had the nerve to call. Had he finished loving his girlfriend and now wanted a conversation with her? She ignored the call and poured herself a glass of wine instead. She started the dishwasher and then climbed the stairs to her bedroom. She turned on her stereo and listened to Jill

Scott serenade her with an appropriate song, a remake of Billie Holiday's "Good Morning Heartache," while Chris Botti accompanied her with his horn. She drew a hot bath, climbed in and relaxed her head against the tub.

She tossed and turned all night, and even when the sunlight flashed across her face in the morning, she wanted to lie there just a little longer. Unfortunately, she needed to get Chloe dressed and ready for school, so wallowing in her misery was not an option. She needed to drop Chloe off and then head over to her office to pack up her things. Staying in West Palm Beach was no longer in the cards. She needed a one-way ticket to London by week's end. She pulled herself out of bed.

"Let's go, sweetheart. In the shower you go," Savannah told Chloe.

"Can I stay home today, Mommy?"

"Are you sick?"

"I'm really tired."

Savannah felt her head for a fever. They'd had a long weekend, and Savannah concluded that she was just tired from their trip to the Bahamas.

"Okay, kiddo. You can hang out with Mommy today. I have to go to my office and pack my things. And I just need for you to behave. Okay?"

"Okay," she said. "Are we going to see Daddy today, too?"

"I don't think so, honey. I'm sure your dad has to work."

"Can we see him after he gets off work?"

Savannah sighed. How was she going to avoid Edward for an entire week? "We'll see."

Maia stood in the doorway of Savannah's office. A tight blue dress hugged her ample hips.

"So...we're back from the islands."

"Yes, we are."

"And did we have a good time?"

"We did indeed."

"Did we get some of that big, fat, sexy..."

"Maia! Chloe's here."

Chloe popped up from behind her mother's desk, a Barbie doll in her hand.

"Damn, I didn't even see her over there." Maia covered her mouth. "Hi, sweetheart. How are you?"

"Hi, Maia." Chloe waved.

"That's a cute little Barbie you have there." Maia smiled sheepishly. "What's her name?"

Chloe shrugged. "Barbie."

Savannah dug into her purse for some change, pulled out four quarters.

"Baby, why don't you run down the hall and get something out of the vending machine. Let Mommy talk to Maia." She handed Chloe the change.

"Okay." Chloe left the office and closed the door behind her.

"I'm headed to London this weekend," Savannah whispered.

"What?" Maia said. "What about your text message? You said that you and what's his name had found love again...or some nonsense. And you were considering putting London on hold for a while."

"That was before."

"What happened?"

"We weren't back in the country two hours and that tramp was already at his house, in his bed."

"What!" Maia's eyes grew large as she eased her behind into the chair across from Savannah's desk. "How do you know?"

"Her car was parked in front of his house. Plus I called

him, and she answered his cell phone. Said that he was in the shower and the two of them were about to go to bed together."

"She was lying!"

"She wasn't lying."

"She has wanted him since the beginning of time. You know that. She would do anything to get rid of you and get her claws into him."

"I, um..." Savannah hadn't considered that Quinn might be lying. But how did she have access to his phone? And more importantly, why was he in the shower while she was there? She didn't care anymore. She'd cried herself to sleep the night before, and she didn't have any more tears for Edward Talbot. It was time to get down to the business at hand. "I need you to take Chloe for me."

"What!"

"Just for a few weeks. Just until the end of the school year and until I get settled in London."

"Savannah, are you insane? I don't know anything about taking care of a five-year-old."

"You just have to make sure she gets to school every day. Feed her and put her to bed every night. Chloe's easy to care for and she knows our routine very well."

"And what happens when her father calls and demands to see her?" Maia asked. "Savannah, why don't you just leave her with Edward for a while...at least until you get settled?"

"I don't know."

"He'll take better care of her than I will. Trust me. I don't even have pets or plants, for Christ's sake!"

Savannah plopped down in her leather chair. This wasn't going to be as easy as she thought. But Maia had a point. Edward was good with Chloe. He would take great care of her, at least until the end of the school year. And once she got settled in London with Nyle, she'd come back for her daughter.

The door opened and Chloe came back in.

"I might give him a chance," said Savannah.

"How about giving him a chance to explain, too." Maia stood, headed for the door.

"Now you're on his side?"

"Never," Maia said. "But you should at least hear his side of the story."

"Now you're pushing it."

"Am I?" Maia asked. "Check in with me before you leave."

"I will."

Savannah continued to place pictures and other personal items into the cardboard box. Leaving was proving to be much harder than she'd anticipated.

Chapter 17

Edward refused to leave Savannah's house until he saw her pull up. He'd been worried sick, wondering if she and Chloe were okay. He'd been calling her cell phone and work phone for two days, and so far she hadn't picked up and hadn't returned one single call. He saw her sedan in his rearview mirror as she crept down the street. She pulled into the driveway and he stepped out of the car. He went to his trunk and grabbed the black leather luggage that belonged to her.

He stood on the lawn, his arms folded across his chest, waited for her to get out of the car. Chloe wasn't in the car, and his heart beat rapidly. Where was his daughter?

"Hey." He frowned, although a feeling of relief rushed over him. At least she was unharmed, but he was still a bit angry that he hadn't heard from her and she hadn't returned any of his calls or text messages. "Where's Chloe?"

"She's having a playdate with one of the little girls from our church." She grabbed a box from the front seat of her car.

"Let me carry that for you."

"I got it. Thanks."

"I brought your bag. We got the two mixed up the other night." He grabbed the bag by its handle.

"I know."

"Is something wrong here?"

"You tell me."

"I've been calling you for the past two days, and you haven't picked up, haven't returned any of my calls," he said. "What's going on?"

"I've been busy." She placed the box on the ground and opened her front door.

"Why aren't you using the garage?"

"The garage door opener went out last week."

"It's not safe. You should be pulling into the garage instead of going in through the front door," he stated as he followed her into the house. "I'll fix it."

"It's okay. I won't be here long anyway. Leaving for London very soon."

"What? When were you going to tell me?"

"I wasn't." She set the box down at the edge of the stairs, went to the corner and grabbed his luggage by the handle and wheeled it toward him. "But then I realized that I need your help. Chloe's got a few more weeks of school left..."

"Six weeks," Edward added.

"Anyway, I don't want to pull her out of school. So I'd like for you to take her, just for a few weeks until school's out and I get settled. Find a place..."

"Why are you leaving? I thought..." He chose his words carefully. "I thought you might reconsider after..."

"After what, Edward? After you made me believe that we could really have a future together?"

"We *can* have a future together," he insisted.

Had she figured it out? That in the beginning, his intentions had been to romance her into staying?

"We can't have a future!" She raised her voice. "Not when you're still seeing other people and sleeping with them! I'm not into casual sex, and I won't be your side chick."

"What in the hell are you talking about, Savannah?"

"I'm talking about Quinn."

"Not that again."

"Yes, that again!" She looked at him in disgust. "So, for your information, I'm not interested in a future with you, Edward Talbot. I am fine with my life…just the way it is. The only thing I need from you is a father for my child. I need for you to care for her until I come back for her in a few weeks."

"I haven't given you permission to take her away," said Edward.

"I don't need your damn permission! If I wanted to, I'd take her in the middle of the night without your knowledge. But I'm being respectful here," she stated.

"We have joint custody, so you do need my permission!" he exclaimed.

"We're going to London, with or without your blessing."

"And how will you obtain a passport for her? With the help of the criminal who texted your phone while we were in the Bahamas?"

"Were you spying on me? Sneaking around, checking my phone?"

"Answer the question. Is that what your plans are?"

"No. You'll sign the application. You and I will both sign the application," she said.

"What makes you so certain that I will?"

"Would you really deny your daughter the opportunity to live with her mother? She would be miserable without me, and you know it. No one can take care of Chloe better than me. Of course, you're her father, but a girl shouldn't be without her mother. I know that firsthand!"

It was true and he knew it. Savannah had grown up without her mother, and it had nearly destroyed her. She'd never been a whole person, and he'd always felt bad for her. He didn't want that for Chloe.

"When are you planning to leave?" he asked.

"End of the week," she said.

It felt as if the wind had left his soul. "End of the week?"

"Friday evening. And I'll be back to get her the minute that school's out. I should be settled by then."

"And once you come back for her, and the two of you are settled in London, how will I see Chloe?"

"I'll send her to you on breaks and during the summer. Not Christmas. I need her during the Christmas holidays. But you can have any other holidays you want."

Edward felt deep sadness and an aching in his heart. What had caused Savannah's sudden change of heart? He was sure when they had returned from the Bahamas that her intentions had been to stay in Florida. They were supposed to be engaged by the end of the week, not moving to London. This was all wrong.

"Fine." His voice cracked and he tightened his jaw. He wouldn't show her his emotions. He would shield his hurt and anger. "Will you sell the house?"

"Yes. I have the card for that real estate agent that we met with before. I'll get in contact with her."

"I'll work with her to get it on the market. She can call me for showings and such."

"Thank you." She remained in her professional mode. "That will help me quite a bit. Not to have to worry about that."

"I'll continue to pay the mortgage until it sells." He looked around at the home they'd built from the ground up.

"That's very generous, Edward. And I appreciate everything that you do for Chloe."

"And for you, Savannah. I do them for you as well. I love you both." There. He'd said it. He loved her. He walked toward the door, felt like he couldn't breathe. He stood there for a moment, his shoulders sunken. He felt defeated, but the words he was about to speak would be the hardest ones he ever had to say. "I don't know what happened between Sunday and today, but I'm sorry for whatever it was. And I hope that you'll be very happy in London. I won't give you any trouble about taking Chloe. As long as I can still see her during breaks and holidays, as you've promised."

"You'll see her. We can go before a judge and get it in writing."

"I'll have Jack draw something up," he stated.

"Fine."

He grabbed his luggage, walked out while he was still able. Headed straight for his car and didn't turn around. He popped the trunk and tossed the bag inside. Slid into the driver's seat, started the car and sat there for a moment. He was numb. Felt as though he couldn't move. He grabbed the steering wheel tightly and shook it. He glanced at her door. She'd already closed it.

He drove to Jupiter Beach and pulled into the lot. He needed some air, to breathe, to think. Still wearing slacks and dress shoes, he got out of the car. He didn't even bother to remove his expensive tan-and-brown loafers. He walked through the sand and didn't care. He didn't care that he smelled rain, or that thunder roared and lightning flashed across the sky. Beachgoers were packing up their things and heading for their cars. People were pulling their Jet Skis in from the ocean.

A few raindrops pattered against his face. He kept

walking until the sky opened and a flood of rain poured over him. He didn't care. He needed to cry, and this was the perfect time to do it. This way the trace of his tears could be concealed by the raindrops. And he did it. He cried. Long and hard.

Chapter 18

Trying to reconnect with Edward had been a mistake. For Savannah, there had always been a void in her life that only Nyle could fill. Reconnecting with her mother was something that she needed. London was also the perfect place to nurture her career in fashion design. She and Edward had connected in the Bahamas, but she wasn't willing to change her plans. Not this time. It was time for her career and her own plans. As hard a decision as it was to leave Chloe, she didn't have many choices. She wasn't certain of her own future in London, and wouldn't bring Chloe along until she had some level of stability. She vowed that once she found a job in fashion and a place, she'd come back for her daughter. And she didn't have a huge window of time; six weeks would fly by.

Before Savannah boarded her flight to London, tears streamed down her face. She stared out the window as she waited for them to announce that they were boarding, rain pouring down outside. It had rained all week, and she wondered if it was washing away her past, giving her a fresh start. She wanted to be excited about her venture, but the truth was, she was sad. Leaving Chloe had been brutal, and watching her daughter cry as she pulled away in a cab had been pure torture. She only hoped that she could manage without her.

She knew that Edward was a good father, but he'd never had Chloe on his own. Though it was only temporary, there would be sacrifices that Edward would have to make, and she wasn't sure that he would be able to make them—ones that he hadn't made in their marriage. He would have to get his priorities in order. She wasn't so sure that Edward could manage that. But deep in her heart, she hoped that he could—for their daughter's sake.

Once she was situated in the leather seat on the plane, she knew there was no turning back. It was real. In about fourteen hours, with a two-hour layover in Atlanta, she'd be there. She'd be knocking on her mother's door and staring into her eyes. She hoped they would bond quickly, and that it wouldn't be too awkward. She hoped to be employed soon and living on her own. Thanks to Edward's paying her mortgage since the divorce, she had been able to save up a nice little nest egg—one that would get her through until she was able to land a new job. And not just any job. She wanted to work at one of those London fashion design companies that she'd only read about in magazines. She had gained a great deal of experience in the fashion industry since working for Jarrod. Her resume was polished and she was ready to take the industry by storm.

She placed her phone on airplane mode, leaned her head back against the seat and closed her eyes. Whispered a little prayer for safe travels.

"First time in the UK?" asked the handsome man in the seat next to hers.

"I was there when I was a baby. I don't remember it, though," she said.

"Business or pleasure?" he asked in his British accent.

"A little of both."

"How long are you staying?"

He was full of questions, she thought.

"Indefinitely," she said. "I'm relocating."

"Well, welcome home," he held his hand out to her. "I'm Rolf."

"Savannah." She shook his hand.

"Already found a place to stay?" he asked.

"With my mother," she said.

"Ooh. Mommy dearest. My condolences."

"What's that supposed to mean?"

"Nothing. Your mother is probably a very sweet woman and easy to live with." He laughed. "Mine, on the other hand…a piece of work."

"I don't really know my mother," she said. "Long story."

"Well, if you find yourself in the market for a place to stay, I have a two-bedroom flat for rent in South Kensington. You can walk to museums. Seven minutes to the Tube…"

"The Tube?"

"The rail station," he said, handing her a business card. "I usually rent it out short-term, but I'm open to a long-term renter. Give me a call if you'd like to see it."

"Thanks. But I think I'll be okay." She slid the card into a pocket on her cell phone case.

"Great. Let's hope." Rolf gave Savannah a gentle smile and then plugged his earbuds into his ears, began to listen to music on his iPad.

Savannah opened the photo gallery on her phone. Looked at pictures of Chloe. She'd only been away from her daughter a short time and already had separation anxiety. She didn't know how she'd make it through the next few weeks without her. The pilot finally leveled the plane and Savannah relaxed in her seat. She reached into her leather backpack and pulled out the romance novel she'd packed for the trip. Romance was definitely not on her mind, but she needed something to help pass the time. Before the second chapter, she'd already begun to doze.

Nyle was supposed to pick her up at the airport, but left a text message that something had come up. She gave instructions on how to get to her place, and to go ahead and take care of the taxi—she'd be reimbursed the moment she arrived. The Peugeot E7's engine hummed at the curb of Heathrow Airport, and Savannah slid into the backseat of the black cab. She gave the driver Nyle's address and relaxed on the right side of the car behind him. He glanced at her in the rearview mirror, his face expressionless. She looked away and took in the picturesque views of the city.

While she was used to driving on the right side of the street in America, the Londoner taxi driver maneuvered the car along the left side—much like the drivers in the Bahamas. In fact, the British and Bahamians had quite a bit in common, Savannah thought, remembering riding on the opposite side of the street when she visited the Bahamas. Though the queen of England was not involved in the day-to-day business of the Bahamas government, she was still its queen.

Visiting Buckingham Palace was definitely on Savannah's list of things to do. She wanted to get all of her touristy type things out of the way before she became a permanent fixture. But for now, she needed a long, hot bubble bath or at least a shower. And just as her stomach growled, she wondered if Nyle had a nice meal waiting, too. She was exhausted, but excited about being there and thrilled to meet the woman who gave her life. All of the anger and hostility that she'd felt in the past had suddenly been replaced by intrigue and curiosity. She still hadn't completely forgiven her, but she was open to other emotions.

Savannah paid the driver with cash and found herself on Nyle's doorstep ringing the bell for much longer than she thought necessary. Wasn't the woman expecting her? It seemed she should've been standing with the door wide open, waiting for her daughter with outstretched arms. She thought that Nyle should've met her at the cab and helped her carry her bags inside. After having no luck with ringing the bell, she knocked.

"She stepped out for a moment," yelled the neighbor from the doorway of her flat. "Said she'd be back shortly."

"Are you freaking kidding me?" Savannah mumbled under her breath. But then gave the red-haired neighbor a wave. "Thank you."

"You're the daughter, eh?"

"Yes, ma'am."

"You're pretty like her. You're not licentious, too, are you?"

"Licentious?" asked Savannah.

"A loose woman," the neighbor said. "Like your mother."

"I'm not loose. But thank you for asking," said a tired Savannah to the busybody neighbor. She seemed to have a few loose screws.

She glanced down the narrow street and knew that the woman rushing down the block toward her was Nyle. With a grocery bag in one hand and a cigarette in the other, she was easy to recognize. She walked like Savannah. Had the same build, but just a bit more developed. She wore black leather pants that were much too tight for a woman her age, thigh-high boots and a black leather jacket. Her brown hair was shoulder-length and a pair of red-lensed glasses covered her olive-colored face. She was attractive and definitely had her own style.

"Have you been waiting long?" Nyle asked as she approached, a huge smile on her face. Her teeth were starting to brown. Undoubtedly from the cigarette smoking.

"Not very."

"Look at you! You're stunning," she said. "You don't look anything like your photographs. Isn't she stunning, Harriett?"

"Gorgeous," the busybody neighbor, Harriett, murmured through a raspy, cigarette-filled cough. "Did you bring the smokes?"

Nyle reached into her pocket and pulled out a package of cigarettes, tossed them to Harriett. "You should smoke the herbal ones. They're free of nicotine, and strawberry-flavored."

"What would be the point?"

Nyle ignored her. She didn't hug Savannah but wrapped an arm around her shoulder as if they were old friends who hadn't missed the past thirty-plus years together. "Let's go inside and catch up."

Savannah looked around at the beautifully decorated flat and thought that the money that she'd sent Nyle had been put to good use. White leather furniture, and glass fixtures were everywhere. A fuzzy rug was the focal point in the center of the room, and intriguing art adorned the walls.

"Nice place," Savannah said thoughtfully.

"Thanks. But I can't take the credit. Godfrey has quite the style." She placed the grocery bag in the kitchen and then plopped down on the sofa.

"Godfrey?"

"My boo," she said. "Isn't that what you youngsters are calling them these days?"

Savannah shrugged. Still standing. Purse on her shoulder. “I can’t say that I use that term. So this isn’t your place?”

“It’s Godfrey’s place. He lets me bunk here while he travels the world. He’s very well off,” said Nyle, and then she quickly changed the subject. “How’s your father?”

Savannah wondered just how long she’d known Godfrey, and why she hadn’t rushed to him for refuge when she was put out on the street. And what Nyle had done with the rent money she’d wired to her. She wanted to ask, but decided to let it go.

“Daddy’s doing well,” Savannah said. “He’s retired now.”

“Gorgeous military man. Ex-military man. He swept me off my feet, Frank did. He was always so grounded. Regimented. Not like me. I was a free spirit,” she said. “Sit down.”

Savannah slid onto the edge of the white leather chair. “Thank you.”

“You’re so polite. Just like him. You’re nothing like me. You have my good looks, though.” She smiled. “But nothing else. He did well with you.”

“Yes, he did.”

“Tell me about yourself. I know over the phone, you told me that you went to college in Florida.”

“Florida State. And then I went to art school in Savannah.”

“You were named after that city, you know. Such a beautiful place. Those cobblestone streets… Go on.” She giggled. “I interrupted.”

“I have a degree in fashion, and before last week…a job.”

“You’ve definitely come to the right place. London is the fashion capital of the world.”

“Not anymore. It’s New York now.”

"Whatever," said Nyle as she lit another herbal cigarette. "It's a close second. A good place to plant your feet in the fashion industry."

"Right."

"I used to be in fashion myself. I was a model in my younger days. I've graced the covers of *Vogue* and *L'Officiel* magazines."

"Seriously?"

"You didn't know?" she asked. "It's why I couldn't take you along. It's why your father and I parted ways. I was traveling too much, trying to pursue my career. He didn't understand."

"You mean you chose your career," Savannah said matter-of-factly.

"I wanted to bring you here to England, with me. But your father wouldn't allow it."

Savannah became uncomfortable with the way the conversation was headed. She wasn't ready to face the past just yet. She was tired. And hungry. And not at all ready for truths about her childhood. She wasn't ready to defend her father, nor let Nyle off the hook for her misgivings either. She needed a good night's rest before she contended with the heavy issues.

"Is there somewhere I can freshen up?"

"Yes, of course. Follow me." Nyle led the way down a long hallway.

She flipped on the light in one of the bedrooms. "This is where you'll be sleeping. You can place your things in here. And the toilet is just down there on the right."

"Thanks," said Savannah.

"I'm going to prepare something to eat for us. We'll have Cumberland pie. Have you had that before?"

"No. Can't say that I have."

"Good. You'll love it." Nyle placed a gentle hand on her daughter's cheek. "I'm glad you're here."

"Me, too."

"And when you're done…freshening up…you can tell me all about Chloe, and Edward. If you want to talk about him. I know he's the ex. So we don't have to talk about him at all, if you don't want to. But Chloe… I want to know all about her."

"I'll tell you all about her once I get settled."

"Fantastic." She smiled.

Savannah took note of how beautiful Nyle was. She could picture her face gracing the cover of fashion magazines once upon a time. She wanted to talk to her about life, and catch up on all that they'd missed, but for now—she needed a moment to catch her breath. And sleep.

Chapter 19

Edward struggled to get the rubber band around Chloe's thick ponytail. The center part was crooked, and the second ponytail was more flyaway than the first one, but he'd managed to complete the task. He'd combed Chloe's hair. He was happy that it was Saturday and she didn't have school. At least he'd have the weekend to practice before Monday morning.

"There!" he said with pride. "It's not quite like Mommy's, but it's done. Go look in the mirror."

Chloe hopped down from the kitchen bar stool and rushed down the hall to the bathroom. Edward cleaned up the mess he'd made with ribbons, bows and other hair products. He grabbed the remote control for his stereo and turned the volume up. Washed his hands and began to season the orange roughy he and Chloe had picked up at the farmers' market. His cell phone rang.

"Hello."

"It's me." Savannah's voice was music to his ears. "How are things going?"

He tried to hide his excitement. "Everything's fine."

"Where's Chloe?"

"She's in the bathroom looking at her hair. Daddy combed it today."

"Oh, Lord."

"What? I did a good job. She looks great."

"Well, let me ask her for myself," said Savannah.

"How was your trip?" Edward asked. "I'm glad you made it safely."

"It was long and tiring. When I made it to Nyle's place, I was exhausted and hungry."

"What's she like?" he asked in an almost-whisper, as if Nyle could hear him.

Savannah giggled. "Somewhat eccentric. Pretty, though."

"I understand why you needed to go, Savannah. I do. I know how important this is."

"Thank you. I needed to hear that."

"Let me get Chloe," said Edward as he walked to the bathroom where Chloe stood on the toilet and gazed at her hair in the mirror. "Sweetheart, your mother's on the phone."

"Mommy!" Chloe exclaimed and then hopped down from the toilet. She grabbed the phone from Edward's grasp.

Edward walked out of the bathroom. Gave them a bit of privacy and an opportunity to catch up. He hoped that Chloe wouldn't resort to crying again after hanging up the phone. She had cried the entire day before and most of the night. She was more attached to Savannah than he imagined. He guessed that every girl felt that way about her mother, but it left him helpless.

He stepped out back and placed charcoal briquettes in the grill, fired it up. Chloe rushed outside and handed him the cell phone and then bolted back into the house.

He looked at the screen and realized that Savannah was still on the line.

"Hello."

"She's sad, but she'll be okay later," Savannah explained. She was tearful. "I miss her like crazy. I hope I can do this."

"She'll be fine. You don't have to worry, Savannah. I promise I'll take great care of our daughter."

"I know. And I'll be okay," she sniffed. "I'm just fatigued and emotional."

"Get some rest, and visit with your mother. We'll give you a call in a couple of days and check on you," said Edward. "Let's not run up your phone bill. Hit us up on Facebook."

"Okay."

"I'll post pictures of Chloe every day, so that you can feel like you're a part of her routine."

"Okay." She smiled. "Thank you."

"My pleasure. Now go get some rest and check your Facebook page later. I'll post pictures of her hair."

Savannah laughed through her tears. "I can only imagine what it looks like."

"Like I told you before, it looks great. You'll see," he said. "Now I have to go. Gotta get this fish on the grill."

"Okay. Kiss her for me."

"I will. We'll talk soon."

Edward wanted to ease her anxiety as best he could, and when he hung up he felt as if he'd been successful.

He and Chloe sat in front of the television, ate fish and watched a Disney movie. He wanted to ignore the text message that he received from his colleague, asking if he'd completed his part of the report for Sunday morning's presentation. The mayor was meeting with one of the city's top officials for Sunday brunch, and she needed her talking points. He hadn't finished them. He'd rushed out of the office on Friday and headed straight for Chloe's school because he needed to be on time picking her up. He'd completely forgotten about the report and the meeting.

"Damn," he mumbled under his breath.

He glanced over at his daughter, dressed in her *Sofia the First* pajamas. He hated the thought of loading her into the backseat of his car and dragging her into the office on a Saturday night, but he didn't have much of a choice. Duty called. He'd have completed the report using his laptop computer, but he needed access to the files in his office.

"Baby, we're going to take a ride," he told her.

"Where?"

"To Daddy's office," he said. "I need for you to go find some shoes and to pack some toys into your backpack."

"Okay, Daddy." She rushed down the hallway and was back in a few moments.

He pulled out of his Delray Beach subdivision and zoomed down Atlantic Avenue, then pulled onto Interstate 95 toward downtown West Palm Beach. The sun was already beginning to set as the palm trees swayed in the wind, and he hoped to be back soon and have Chloe in bed at a decent hour.

In his office, Chloe sat in a chair and spread her toys out across his mahogany desk. He pulled files from the cabinet and began flipping through their pages, turned on his computer. He plugged numbers into an Excel spreadsheet, then found music on his iPad.

When he glanced at the clock again, it was well after midnight. Chloe had since curled up and fallen asleep. He leaned back in his chair. Exhausted. He grabbed his cell phone and pulled up the camera, snapped a shot of Chloe's hair, then logged into Facebook and sent it in a message to Savannah. She immediately replied.

What took you so long? And where is she?

At my office. I had work to finish up.

On a Saturday night?

Yes.

It's after midnight!

He'd made a mistake, snapping the photo at his office. He knew that Savannah would worry about things that she had no business worrying about. But she was the one who'd left him in this predicament.

We're headed home now.

It wasn't completely a lie. All he needed was another thirty minutes or so and he'd be homeward bound. He put the finishing touches on his report, pulled charts and graphs into his spreadsheet, and saved the document. After this, he shut down his computer. He glanced over at Chloe and a wave of guilt rushed over him. She was supposed to be at home tucked into bed. What type of father kept his little girl out until the wee hours of the morning? He brushed sleep from his own eyes, turned off the music and then lifted Chloe into his arms. He turned off the lights and carried her out to the parking lot.

Chapter 20

Savannah ordered porridge with a fruit salad, while Nyle went for the full breakfast with eggs Florentine and American-style pancakes with fresh fruit and maple syrup, and steak frites. She insisted on a Bloody Mary to top it all off. Snagging a table at Balthazar London was usually very difficult, but for Sunday morning brunch they had no problem. The French brasserie was a perfect imitation of New York's version of the restaurant, with red awnings, red leather banquettes, huge antiqued mirrored walls and mosaic floors.

Savannah watched in awe as Nyle ate as though there was no tomorrow. It had been her idea that the two eat there. Nyle insisted on treating Savannah to a nice English meal at her favorite brunch spot. She spent the entire meal catching Savannah up on all that had taken place in her life over the years. She shared the story of how she met Godfrey, the man she'd been in a relationship with for the past few weeks.

"He's a wonderful lover," she stated, "but he's never home. Always traveling abroad. The flat is his. I just lay my head there."

"Does he know that I'm staying there?"

"Of course."

"Are you sure?" Savannah pressed.

Nyle gave a nod. "We're two ships in the night. Our paths rarely cross."

"Why do you put up with that? Why not find a man who has time for you?"

"I like him," she said. "And I enjoy the time to myself when he's gone."

"I guess if it works for you both. How does he feel about it?"

She laughed. "He has the nerve to be jealous."

"Will you ever marry?" Savannah asked.

"Doubtful. We're fine this way. Why fix something that isn't broken?" Nyle asked. "Marriage is overrated anyway. I've been down that road before, and so have you. Will you ever remarry?"

"I don't know. I suppose if the right man comes along." Savannah finished her porridge. "Edward and I spent some time together in the Bahamas recently. I thought we might reconcile, but it didn't really work out."

"Why not?" asked Nyle.

Savannah looked at her mother. Wasn't ready to share everything with her just yet. They needed to build trust.

"Timing."

"What does that mean? You weren't ready or he wasn't?"

"Neither of us. "

"Another woman?"

"Where did you get that idea?"

"It's obvious. You seem scorned," said Nyle. "Was he not worth fighting for?"

"We're not married anymore. We both have moved on," said Savannah. "Now let's drop it."

Nyle raised her hands in surrender. "It's dropped."

After the server brought the check, Nyle grabbed it from the table and then dug into her purse. "I thought I had a few bloody pounds in here. I must've left them on the table at home."

"Don't worry about it. I have my MasterCard." Savannah grabbed the check from Nyle. "I'll take care of it."

"I'll give it back as soon as we get home."

"No worries," said Savannah, and she paid the check.

The pair hopped into the backseat of a hackney carriage. Nyle slid in first and hugged the driver from behind. "Where the hell have you been, you ornery man?" she asked the blond-haired older man.

"I've been bloody working!" The driver glanced at Savannah in the rearview mirror, and then gave Nyle a wide grin.

"This is my daughter," Nyle explained.

"Wow! Really. She's just as beautiful as you are," he said. "You don't look old enough to have a daughter that old."

"Savannah, this is Xander. Xander, Savannah."

"Pleasure meeting you, Savannah," said Xander. "You're not from here, are you?"

"No."

"Will you be staying long?"

"I hope so."

"Savannah has relocated from the US."

"I see," Xander said as he glanced at Savannah again. "Welcome. I think you'll find it a wonderful place to live. What part of town are you looking at?"

"She's living with me for the time being," Nyle explained. "At least until she gets her feet grounded."

Xander slammed on the brake to avoid hitting the car in front of him. He was distracted—too busy staring at Nyle in the rearview. When he pulled up in front of the Design Museum, Savannah exhaled. His driving made her nervous. Savannah and Nyle hopped out of the car. They took in the industrial and fashion design that the museum had to offer. They shopped for jewelry and had coffee at the little café that overlooked the Thames. They talked about fashion, and when they were done taking in the exhibitions, they walked out and found Xander, who was waiting with the car running. They visited three more museums.

Nyle had Xander stop at a liquor store, where she sent him in for a bottle of wine. And soon he pulled the car in front of Nyle's flat. Savannah opened her purse to look for a few pounds to pay for the cab ride. Nyle placed a hand over Savannah's and shook her head no. She snapped her purse shut.

"Thank you, Xander," Nyle said.

"My pleasure." Xander gave Nyle a wink in the mirror and waited for the ladies to exit the cab.

Savannah stepped out first and waited for her mother. Nyle whispered something to Xander, patted him on the shoulder and then exited the cab. Xander grinned at whatever was said and then slowly pulled away from the curb. Nyle hooked her arm inside Savannah's as they walked up to the front door.

"What a fun day," she exclaimed.

"I enjoyed it," Savannah agreed. "You and Xander must be pretty close."

"We're old chums," said Nyle as she unlocked the door. "Now let's get that bottle of wine opened, kick our shoes off and have some girl talk."

The thought of it sounded good to Savannah. She went to her room and pulled flannel pajamas out of her bag. She hadn't completely unpacked. There was still some reservation from before, but she was starting to relax a bit more. She removed her underwear from her luggage and placed it in the top bureau drawer. She then put her socks and shirts in the middle drawer. She hung clothes in the closet. She grabbed her toothbrush and pajamas and headed down the hall to the bathroom. Turned on the shower. She desperately needed a shower.

As the water cascaded over her naked body, she thought of Edward. His touch and the way he had kissed her lips and made love to her on the beach. She missed Chloe, but had to admit that part of her missed Edward, too. She admitted that to herself, though she had no intentions of admitting it to anyone else. She wished with all her heart that she could get him out of her head. She had presumed that once she arrived in London, she could actually rid her thoughts of him. She didn't expect to think of him more.

She dried herself off with a thick towel and sat on the edge of the tub. Grabbed her cell phone and logged on to Facebook. Edward had posted pictures of Chloe, and Savannah smiled as she scrolled through them. She even smiled at the selfie that Edward and Chloe had taken together, both of them sticking their tongues out and crossing their eyes. They appeared to be having fun together, and Savannah's heart was filled with envy.

"Nice photos," she typed.

We're watching a movie.

Shouldn't she be preparing for bed?

No. We're about five hours behind you.

Savannah had forgotten about the time difference.

Did she complete homework? Make sure she has a bath. And make sure she brushes her teeth.

We got this. How was your day with Nyle?

Surprisingly wonderful. We're about to have wine and girl talk.

That should be fun.

Maybe.

Well, don't worry about us. We're good. Go have fun and we'll talk tomorrow.

Okay. Gn.

Gn Savannah.

She washed her face, brushed her teeth, and slipped into her pajamas. When she opened the bathroom door, loud music resonated through the flat—Jimi Hendrix sang "Purple Haze" and the stench of marijuana drifted in the air.

"Is she serious?" Savannah whispered to herself.

She walked to her room and grabbed her bathrobe, wrapped it around her body and tightened the belt. She crept down the hall and into the living area to see what Nyle was up to. She peeked around the corner and Nyle was sitting in the easy chair in the corner of the room, a glass of wine in one hand and a joint in the other. She took a long drag from the joint and leaned her head back in slow motion. Xander had returned and was sitting across the room from Nyle. Laughter filled the air.

So much for girl talk, Savannah thought. She walked back to her room, pulled the door shut and sat in the middle of the bed. She took a novel out of her backpack and started to read.

Chapter 21

Edward was having a hard time balancing his career and Chloe. Handling her alone had become a challenge, but he would never give Savannah the satisfaction of knowing that.

He pulled into the parking lot of the elementary school. Chloe and Miss Jennings sat on the steps. He hopped out of the car and rushed toward them.

"I'm so sorry, Miss Jennings. I had a late meeting," he explained.

"How are you, Mr. Talbot?" Miss Jennings's usual flirty smile wasn't there. She had an edge of disappointment in her voice. "We've been waiting for almost an hour."

"I'm sorry. I promise it won't happen again," he said, and grabbed Chloe by the hand. He threw the strap of her backpack over his shoulder.

She gave him a smile. "Please see that it doesn't, Mr. Talbot."

He smiled at her brown face and hoped she realized that he really *was* sorry. She gave him a look of disappointment, one that she might give one of her kindergartners when they misbehave. He was grateful that she hadn't read him his rights or threatened to take some action.

"Her mother is away, and I'm doing this on my own."

"I understand," she said. "Her homework is in her backpack."

"Thanks."

"And don't forget to bring her cookies for the celebration tomorrow."

"Cookies?" Edward asked.

"Yes. Each of the kids is bringing a snack for our little celebration. They have to prepare it themselves…with the help of a parent, of course. There was a note about it in her backpack last week."

"I didn't see it. I missed it," said Edward.

"I told you about it, Daddy," Chloe said. "But you were working."

"It's okay," Edward told Miss Jennings. "We'll bake cookies."

"Well good, then. I'll see you tomorrow, Chloe, bright and early. And don't forget to complete your homework assignment."

"I won't, Miss Jennings."

"Good night, Mr. Talbot." She gave him a semismile that time.

"Good night, Miss Jennings." He gave her a genuine one.

Chloe snapped her seat belt on as Edward pulled out of the parking lot.

"Daddy, you were so late! All of the kids were already gone, and I thought you weren't coming," she whined. "Did you forget about me?"

"Of course not, sweetheart. I would never forget about you. Daddy just had a late meeting and it was hard getting here. Traffic was a son of a b…traffic was bad." He reached into the backseat and grabbed her small hand in his. "I promise to do better. Okay?"

"It's okay, Daddy."

"Forgive me?"

"Yes." She smiled. "Can we go for ice cream now?"

"After dinner," he said. "We gotta figure out how to bake these cookies. Or maybe we could just buy some already baked ones at the Piggly Wiggly. We can put them in a plastic container and everything. Pretend. You don't tell, I won't tell."

"We can't pretend, Daddy. We have to bake them for real."

Edward huffed. "Okay."

Edward rushed to the hardware store. He needed to repair the kitchen sink, which had leaked water all night. The leak would damage the wood in the cabinet, not to mention send his water bill into orbit if he didn't repair it right away. He dropped by McDonald's and grabbed Chloe some chicken nuggets. A feeling of guilt rushed over him. He'd promised himself that he would take better care of her, and at least feed her a healthy diet. She'd eaten frozen fish sticks the day before because he'd run out of time, and pizza the day before that. All thoughts of healthy food had gone out the window.

After patching the leak, Edward and Chloe found themselves at Piggly Wiggly, making it through the automatic doors in just the knick of time. Chloe was already sluggish and winding down, and Edward worried that she wouldn't stay awake long enough to see the cookies to their fully baked state. But Miss Jennings had insisted that the children prepare them themselves.

"I know it's past your bedtime, sweetheart, but you have to stay awake," he warned as they rushed through the express lane. "You have to bake these cookies."

"I know, Daddy."

He grabbed his receipt from the freckle-faced cashier and

picked Chloe up. Carried her to the car. She was sound asleep by the time they pulled into the garage. Edward sat in the car for a moment. He sighed. Wondered how Savannah managed to do all of this by herself—keep house, manage a career and take care of Chloe. All of it was next to impossible for him, yet she made it seem effortless.

Chloe stood on a step stool and placed little squares of chocolate chip cookie dough on the pan. Edward heated the oven, and then placed the cookie sheet inside. He set the timer and then grabbed the television remote, flipped to ESPN, relaxed on the leather sofa. Chloe rested her head in his lap. The cough he'd heard that morning and the night before had returned. She shivered.

"Are you cold, sweetheart?" he asked.

"Yes."

The weather had been mild, and he hadn't turned on the air conditioner for days. Chloe was shivering uncontrollably. He grabbed a throw from the linen closet and wrapped it around her. He felt her forehead, and it was warm.

"You have a slight fever," he announced to her, and went to the bathroom in search of the Children's Tylenol.

"I don't feel good, Daddy."

"What's hurting?" he asked.

"I'm tired," she said. "And my throat hurts from coughing so much."

Savannah would know what to do in situations like this. He wanted to reach out to her, but didn't want to alarm her. Chloe needed Tylenol for the fever and cough syrup for the cough. He found the Tylenol in the medicine cabinet, but not the cough suppressant.

He went to the kitchen and placed the teakettle on the stove. Perhaps a hot cup of tea would do the trick. His phone rang, but he ignored it. Instead grabbed two mugs and two tea bags from the pantry. His phone rang again and he looked at the screen. *Quinn*. He didn't have time to humor her, but he answered anyway. Placed her on speakerphone.

"What's up?" he asked.

"Did you hear the news?"

"What news?"

"Whitman dropped out of the election."

"What?" he said. "No! We need him in the race."

"He's out, dude," said Quinn. "You know what that means, right?"

"What?"

"You have to run," she said. "Stop straddling the fence and make a decision. Just do it."

"I can't right now. Too much going on."

"Oh, right. You're reuniting with Savannah," she said. "How's that going, by the way?"

"It's not." He was frustrated and annoyed. "Quinn, I can't talk right now. I have a sick child and I need to get to the store for a bottle of cough syrup."

"I can drop by the store and grab a bottle of cough syrup for you."

He thought for a moment. As much as he wasn't up for Quinn's company, he hated the idea of dragging Chloe out to the store again even more. The thought of her bringing cough syrup was actually quite appealing.

"That would be great," he said as he pulled burned cookies out of the oven.

"I'll be there shortly."

Quinn held on to Chloe and rocked her to sleep. The coughing had ceased, the fever had gone down and Edward exhaled. He'd panicked, but somehow Quinn had saved the day, and he was grateful.

"I think she's ready for bed now," said Quinn.

Edward stood and lifted Chloe into his arms. He took her to bed and pulled the covers up to her neck. He turned on the humidifier and put the lights down low, then left the door ajar just a bit so that he could hear her. When he returned to the living room, Quinn had made herself comfortable, remote control in hand and flipping through the channels.

"Thank you," he said.

"My pleasure." She smiled.

"You're good with her."

"She's sweet." Quinn made herself at home as she usually did, went into Edward's kitchen and located a bottle of Merlot. She opened it. "Want some wine?"

"Yeah, I'll have a glass." He followed her into the kitchen, pulled two glasses from the cupboard.

"I'm really surprised that Savannah would rush off to London, and leave her daughter like that. Especially when Chloe's not in the best of health," Quinn stated.

"It's not like she just abandoned her. She left her with me, her father."

"I'm not knocking your parenthood, but girls need a mother," she said. "Seems kind of irresponsible."

"She's definitely not irresponsible. She's a great mother."

"Well, you're defensive. Especially since it seems she abandoned you, too," she said. "I thought you were about to propose, and then suddenly she's gone."

"I don't know what happened. I tried calling her that Sunday after we returned from the Bahamas and she never returned my calls. So a few days later I dropped by..." Edward took a sip from his wine.

"To switch the luggage."

"Yeah." A frown on his face, he stared at Quinn. "How did you know that?"

"Know what?"

"That I went there to switch our luggage."

"You told me."

"I never told you that."

"You're mistaken. You told me that you had her luggage and she had yours."

"I never told you that, because I didn't even realize it until the next day. By that time you were long gone. When I opened the suitcase in search of my shaving cream the next morning…" He gave Quinn a look of skepticism. "You have something you want to tell me?"

"No." She wrapped both hands around the bowl of her wineglass, her fingers intertwined.

"What did you do?"

Quinn sighed. "Okay. I might've have answered your phone when you were in the shower."

"You what?" He became angry.

"Savannah called that Sunday when you were in the shower."

"And you answered my phone? Did you also delete the call?"

"I was trying to help you, Edward! You were talking marriage, and proposing…and I know that you're not ready to go down that road again. First of all, if it didn't work the first time, what makes you think that it would work now?"

"Are you out of your mind?"

"No, I'm quite sane," she said. "And did I mention that you should be running for the US Senate…not running around chasing your ex-wife?"

He was livid. Stood and paced the floor. He wanted to make sure he maintained control. He would never strike a woman, but the thought sure crossed his mind. "You have to leave."

"Edward." She giggled. "Don't be silly. It's me, Quinn."

"I'm trying not to throw you out, so I would advise you

to get your ass up and walk out that front door without saying another word to me."

"You're serious?"

He breathed deeply. She was trying his patience. His jaws were tight.

"Damn, you are serious." She finally got it, stood, an inquisitive look on her face. Grabbed her glass of wine and slammed it. She headed for the front door, opened it.

He waited until he heard the door shut before he exhaled. He immediately pulled his cell phone out of his pocket. He needed to reach out to Savannah, explain and apologize profusely. The phone didn't ring. Instead he got her voice mail, and anxiety got the best of him.

He needed to get to her, plead his case. Right the wrongs that Quinn had created. She must've thought him to be a terrible liar and a cheat. He needed her back in the States, so that he could tell her how much he loved her and needed her in his life. He needed to make her his wife and give her the ring that once belonged to her. He was going crazy! A million thoughts rushed through his head.

Chapter 22

Savannah forced her eyes open and glanced at the digital clock on the nightstand. It took her a moment to remember where she was, but she still hadn't quite grasped why she was hearing loud, argumentative voices. She sat straight up in her bed, flipped on the lamp.

"I need you to leave!" a male voice yelled.

Savannah stood, grabbed her robe and wrapped it around her body. She cracked the door a bit and listened.

"I don't have anywhere to go," she heard Nyle say.

"That isn't my problem, now is it?"

"Godfrey! Let me explain."

"I don't need your bloody explanation!"

Savannah crept out of the room, down the hall and into the living room. Xander was standing there in his powder-blue boxer shorts and a white T-shirt that barely covered his large, hairy stomach. A fitted sheet covered Nyle's naked body. Godfrey quickly moved the shotgun from Xander and pointed it at Savannah.

"Hey!" Nyle yelled. "That's my daughter."

Savannah held her hands high in the air. Godfrey moved the gun back to Xander. "Out!" He told him.

Xander reached for his trousers.

"No!" said Godfrey. "Leave them."

"I need my bloody trousers!" Xander complained.

Godfrey cocked the shotgun. "I said leave them!"

Xander rushed toward the front door of the flat and went out into the darkness, half naked.

Godfrey lowered the gun. "I'm leaving. And when I return, I expect you to be packed and gone," he told Nyle.

Within seconds, he was gone. Savannah stared at Nyle. Her eyes begged for an explanation.

"It's okay. No problem," said Nyle.

"What do you mean, no problem?" Savannah asked. "It's after one o'clock in the morning and we're being thrown out on the street?"

"We'll go to Aunt Frances's for the night. Once Godfrey calms down…"

"He doesn't look like he's going to calm down!" Savannah said.

"He will," Nyle explained. "He loves me. He's just really, really mad right now."

"You were sleeping with another man in his home! How will he recover from that?"

"He will." Nyle dropped the sheet, revealing her naked fiftysomething-year-old body that looked more thirtysomething. She began to retrieve her clothing from the floor. "Let's pack an overnight bag."

"I'm packing everything," Savannah said in a huff, and returned to her room.

The pair caught a taxi to Whetstone and pulled up in front of a two-story brick terraced house. They stepped out of the car, bags in tow, and walked up to the door. Before they could knock, the door swung open. An elderly woman stood in the doorway, bent over just a bit, an apron tied around her waist. Her gray hair was pulled back into a ponytail. Her olive face was much like Nyle's.

"Why am I not surprised by your shenanigans?" she asked.

"I don't need your judgment. Just a place to rest my head for the night," Nyle said. "And for my daughter."

"Just for the night, and not a moment longer," said Aunt Frances. "You must be Savannah. You're much prettier in person."

"Thank you." Savannah gave her a half smile. She was still appalled by the events that had led her to this woman's doorstep. "And thank you for letting us stay for the night."

"Come inside. Are you hungry?" She directed her question to Savannah only.

"No, ma'am. Just tired."

"Fine. I'll show you where you'll sleep."

Savannah followed Aunt Frances through the cluttered space with dull hardwood floors and an old brown sofa in the living room. They reached a small bedroom toward the back of the house, and Aunt Frances motioned toward the twin-size bed in the corner.

"Here you are, dear."

"Thank you," Savannah responded and dropped her bags onto the floor. She felt defeated.

"There's a powder room just down the hall."

Savannah nodded her head yes, and within a few seconds Aunt Frances was closing the door behind her. Savannah slipped into a pair of pajamas and then tucked herself beneath fresh-smelling sheets. She wanted to check her Facebook page to see if there were any new postings from Edward. She wanted to talk to him and tell him about everything that had gone on, but her phone had long since died and she hadn't packed her charger. The first chance she got, she needed to find a store that sold mobile phone accessories.

Savannah stared at the ceiling. Wondered how she'd ended up in this chaos called Nyle. She was still quite angry, but giggled at the thought of Xander leaving the flat wearing nothing more than his powder-blue boxers—at gunpoint, nonetheless. She exhaled and before long, sleep captured her and she gave in to it.

Daylight crept through the window and jarred her awake much too soon. Savannah opened her eyes and stared at the ceiling for a moment, tried to grasp where she was. She grabbed her purse and searched inside, found the business card that she'd received from the handsome stranger on the plane—Rolf. She grabbed her robe and wrapped it around her body. Tiptoed out of the room, her bare feet touching the cool floor. Aunt Frances sat at the kitchen table, a newspaper in front of her, reading glasses at the tip of her nose.

"Good morning," she said without even looking up.

"Good morning," said Savannah.

"Coffee is over there." Aunt Frances pointed at the coffeepot on the countertop. "Cups are in cupboard."

"Thanks," Savannah said. "Is there a phone I can use?"

Aunt Frances pointed toward the cordless phone in the corner of the room. "No long-distance calls."

"This is local." Savannah gave her a smile and reached for the phone.

"I mean it. No long distance," Aunt Frances reiterated.

"Yes, ma'am," Savannah simply said and then retreated to her room, dialed Rolf's phone number.

"Yeah," his husky voice answered.

"Rolf?"

"You've got it!"

"We met on the flight from Atlanta to London. Sat next to each other on the plane."

"Savannah," he stated emphatically.

"Yes. You remember."

"Yes, of course," he said. "How's your stay been so far?"

"Well...not so good. Which is why I'm calling. I'd like to see if that flat of yours is still available?"

"Absolutely! When would you like to see it?"

"Right away. Today," she said.

"Fantastic. I can meet you there this afternoon. Say around two?"

"Okay."

"Great. Grab a pen and write down the addy."

She did. Found a pen in the top drawer of the antique chest. She wrote down the address of Rolf's rental property.

"Okay, I got it," she said.

"Take the Tube to the South Kensington station. It's a short stroll from there. The weather is mild, so you should be okay."

"I'll be there at two. Thank you."

Savannah returned the phone to its place in the kitchen.

"If you want breakfast, you'll have to cook it yourself," Aunt Frances said. She hadn't moved from her spot at the table, and she continued to stare at the newspaper. "There's eggs in the refrigerator. Meat. Bread."

"Thank you, but I usually skip breakfast."

"What's your angle here, dear?"

"My angle?"

"Did you come here expecting a happily-ever-after with your mother? Because you certainly won't get it," said Aunt Frances. "She's not capable of doing anything normal. There's not much hope for her, you know?"

Savannah glanced into the living area and noticed that Nyle was on the other side of the wall, listening. She felt sorry for her mother at that moment, and wondered if what Aunt Frances said was true. She wondered if there was any hope for Nyle. After all, she wasn't getting any younger. Savannah averted her eyes as Nyle stepped into the kitchen.

"Morning, ladies," she said and went to the cupboard, grabbed a mug. She poured a cup of coffee.

"Good morning," said Savannah.

Aunt Frances glared at Nyle over the top of her glasses.

Savannah escaped from the kitchen and rushed back down the hall to her temporary quarters. She gathered her underwear and toiletries and retreated to the powder room for a shower. The pipes squealed as she turned on the water. She glanced at herself in the faded mirror and wondered how she'd ended up in this place.

Savannah stepped from the underground train and onto the platform at the South Kensington station. She walked the few short blocks to Rolf's flat, stood outside and waited for him. She was happy to see the black sedan pull up and park in front of the white brick property.

"Been waiting long?" Ray-Ban shades covered Rolf's face.

"Just got here."

"Well, let's go inside."

Shiny hardwood adorned the elegant Victorian flat. A beautiful tan leather sofa and matching chair, glass tables, and stainless appliances made the space look spectacular.

"I'm sure I can't afford this," she stated. "It's already furnished."

"No worries. I'll work with you."

"You do realize I don't have a job, right?" she asked. "I have a couple of months rent, but no job."

"I'll tell you what… I might be able to help. I know that your background is fashion, but I think I might have something that can get you by for a bit." He pulled his wallet from the inside pocket of his blazer. Handed her another business card. "Drop by here. Dr. Abbott. Tell him I sent you. Wear business attire."

She studied the card. "What type of work?"

"It's a receptionist position. It's quite busy, so you'll need to keep up."

"Answering phones?"

"And arranging appointments for a busy doctor. Billing. Things of that nature," he said. "It's a paycheck, right?"

She smiled. "Right."

"I'll take a deposit, but won't charge you rent until you get your first paycheck from Dr. Abbott. However, you're free to move in today if you'd like."

She studied his face. "You're serious."

"Yes."

"You're too kind."

"No smoking and no pets," he warned. "The place rents for nine hundred fifty pounds, but for you rent is six fifty, due on the first, but no later than the fifth."

"How much is that in US dollars?"

"About a thousand US dollars per month."

"I think I can handle that." She grinned.

"I'll draw up a contract," he said. "Is your deposit in cash?"

"Yes. I can switch the currency if you need me to."

"No worries. US dollars are fine."

"Thank you, Rolf. Thank you so much."

"My pleasure." He pulled a single key out of his pocket. Handed it to Savannah. "Welcome home."

In only a few days, she'd snagged her own flat and a new job. Things were quickly looking up.

Chapter 23

Savannah lit a scented candle and found some nice music on the stereo. She'd spent her Saturday morning picking up a few items at a yard sale that she found just a few blocks away. The space couldn't be more perfect, and she tried to make it feel warm, but it felt nothing like home. She missed her house that she and Chloe shared in West Palm Beach. She missed her daughter and their strolls along the beach. She missed picking her up from school and arguing over what to prepare for dinner and helping with homework. She even missed Edward, even though she told herself that she didn't.

She placed an arrangement of fresh flowers in the center of the wooden table and tacked secondhand curtains on the windows. She unpacked her clothes and hung them in the closet, placed her underwear in drawers. She enjoyed her time alone before Nyle returned from picking up groceries. Nyle had settled in, too. She'd claimed the bedroom at the end of the hallway—the one closest to the bathroom. Savannah was reluctant to cohabitate with her again, but knew that her mother had nowhere else to go. She was her only hope. That didn't stop Savannah from reading her the rights—no smoking, no pets and no scandalous behavior, she warned.

It wasn't long before Nyle was banging on the door, her arms filled with bags of food. Savannah let her in and then grabbed the bags, placed them in the kitchen on the counter.

"You bought a lot of stuff."

"Storm's coming," said Nyle. "I want to make sure we have the things that we need."

"That was thoughtful."

"Savannah, I cannot tell you how sorry I am…about all that has gone on," Nyle said. "I promise to make it up to you."

"Don't worry about it," said Savannah. "But I don't want to come home and find you in bed with some random man. I have a five-year-old daughter who will be here soon."

"You don't have to worry about that." Nyle pulled out one of her herbal cigarettes.

"And I said no smoking," Savannah reminded her.

"They're herbal. Not a drop of nicotine in them."

Savannah shook her head no, and Nyle put the cigarette away. In a huff, she started to unpack the groceries. "I'll get dinner started."

Savannah began to help put groceries away in the cupboards and refrigerator. She hoped that she and Nyle could start over again, pretend that nothing ever happened. She wanted this thing to work out, but the truth was, she was afraid to shut her eyes around the woman. She could barely be trusted.

"I almost forgot." Nyle had changed into a pair of the shortest of shorts and a cropped top. Her hair was pulled back into a ponytail. "I picked up a charger for your phone."

Savannah exhaled. "Thank you! Thank you very much."

"I know it's been torture for you, not being able to check in with your little girl."

"I've been going crazy!" Savannah rushed into the bedroom and retrieved her phone, plugged the charger into the wall behind the sofa in the living room.

"You're a good mother. I can tell," Nyle said out of the blue. "A lot better mother than I ever was."

"I made it my business to be in Chloe's life. It's always been my goal."

"You must really trust your ex-husband, to leave your daughter with him."

"I do. He's good with her. He loves her just as much as I do."

"I know you don't like talking about him," said Nyle. "But what went wrong with you two?"

Savannah sighed. Nyle insisted on knowing about Edward, and she wanted to keep her at bay. But then realized that the only way that the two of them would ever get to know each other was to talk about things—things that might be uncomfortable.

"Edward was married to his career. When I was pregnant with Chloe, he was running for mayor. He was never home, always on the campaign trail, and always with his beautiful campaign manager. He barely made it for Chloe's birth."

"Hmmm, another woman," said Nyle. "I bet she wasn't as beautiful as you."

"He claimed that they were just friends. And that nothing ever happened between them."

"But you don't believe it."

"I didn't know what to believe. All I knew was that he hadn't made our marriage a priority. So I rushed to Daddy's house. Hired a lawyer and divorced him."

"Did he fight for you?"

"I think his fight was more about saving face. He was

a political figure, and he didn't want the embarrassment of a divorce."

"But over the years, you two have become friends."

"More like co-parents," said Savannah. "We both have a lot of love for our daughter. We've agreed to be civilized for that reason."

"How does he feel about you moving his daughter to London? How will you pull that off?"

"It wasn't easy, convincing him that this was the right thing to do."

"Is it? The right thing? Because I have to tell you…you don't seem very happy here at all."

Savannah looked at her mother's eyes. Tears threatened to fill hers. Had she been that transparent?

"I know that I've been a terrible mother, Savannah. And I know that you're here looking for all those things that I deprived you of. I know that I left a horrible void in your life. And I'm sorry," Nyle said. "I'm just a rotten person. And I don't know if that will ever change."

"What do you mean?"

"Don't expect too much from me. I'm too old to change." Nyle chuckled. "Don't destroy what you have, the beautiful life that you have, looking for something that might never be."

"What are you saying? It was a mistake to come here?"

"I'm saying that you shouldn't expect too much." Nyle headed into the kitchen. "I'm having a Bloody Mary. You care for one?"

"Sure. Why not?"

After dinner and several Bloody Marys, the women sat in the center of the hardwood floor. Tears filled their eyes as they discussed the difficult issues that they'd avoided until then.

"I hated you," a drunken Savannah revealed. "All of

my friends had mothers who took them shopping and did their hair. I needed you, and you weren't there."

"I know," said Nyle. "My mother did the same bloody thing to me. She wasn't around either. Ran off with some man when I was five. Left me with Aunt Frances to raise me. And I gave that old woman hell!"

"What happened with you two, anyway?" asked Savannah.

"I don't wanna talk about it."

"Oh, come on! I just poured my heart out to you," begged Savannah. "Give me the goods."

"Savannah, I don't want to talk about it."

"What did you do to burn your bridge with Aunt Frances?"

"I didn't do anything!" Nyle exclaimed. She sighed and leaned her head against the edge of the sofa. Her hair was a wild mess on her head. "I'll never forget it as long as I live. I was young, slender like you, beautiful. I was a student at Westminster. Third year. Building my modeling career. Her boyfriend, Felix, came on to me. He'd been drinking... stumbled into my room late one night..."

"Where was Aunt Frances?"

"She worked nights. She was a nurse," Nyle said. "When I told her about it, she didn't believe me. Accused me of being loose, taunting him..."

"Did you? Taunt him?"

"No. He was a disgusting human being. And I did not taunt him. I was promiscuous. I admit that. But I was selective, and I wasn't at all interested in him. Which is why he wanted me so bad." Tears rolled down the side of her face. "She hated me after that. He didn't want her... he wanted me, and she couldn't live with that."

"What happened? Did she ever figure out the truth?"

"He left her for someone else, and she became a bitter old woman. She still blames me, you know."

"Did your mother ever come back?"

Nyle wiped tears from her eyes. "She died when I was seventeen. Committed suicide. Can you believe that? She bloody killed herself!"

Savannah slid across the floor and moved closer to her mother. She grabbed Nyle's hand and held on to it tightly. "I'm sorry."

"You should run away from me as fast as you can. I have nothing in my past but heartache and pain. And nothing good in my future," she said. "You heard what Aunt Frances said about me. It was the truth."

"You never had a chance. You weren't equipped to be a mother," said Savannah. "No one equipped you. Everyone abandoned you."

"Who equipped you?" Nyle asked Savannah.

"No one really. I watched Edward's mother, and I just had instincts. I didn't have a devastating childhood. I was very much loved by my father. And I was just so determined to be a better mother than…"

"…than me."

"It was my driving force," Savannah whispered. "Sorry."

"No apologies necessary. I'm happy that you found hope, Savannah. That you were able to give your daughter what she needed. I never was able to do that."

Savannah rested her head against her mother's bosom. For that moment, she felt as if she truly had a mother.

Chapter 24

Three weeks and Savannah had a new job as a receptionist. It wasn't the job she'd been looking for but it was a job nonetheless. And she had her own flat, and was finding her way about town. But her life wasn't as complete as she thought it would be once she arrived in London. The idea had been to find a career in fashion. And she was grateful to Jarrod for setting up the interview for her with one of the top fashion companies. However, it had been days since she'd met with Herman Mason, and she hadn't received a call back. She feared that she'd be a receptionist much longer than she'd intended to. She also missed Chloe like crazy. She missed their life together—*in Florida*. She missed Maia and her other friends. And though she hated to admit it, she missed Edward.

She looked forward to her daily Facebook chats with him. She'd begun messaging him before and after school. He would post pictures of Chloe and keep her abreast of what they were having for dinner and what homework assignments they were working on. Eventually, the before-and-after-school chats became more frequent. She found herself chatting with Edward throughout the day. The chats weren't just about Chloe, but had become more personal. Soon they'd begun to vent about their workdays. She hoped he hadn't detected the loneliness in her messages.

"Hey, Savannah. We're going out for drinks after work. Why don't you come along?" Mel, her red-haired coworker, stood in front of her. Mel had dipped into the restroom and changed from her professional garb into a short miniskirt with fishnet panty hose.

"No, I'm going to pass." Savannah removed her headset and checked her watch.

"Oh come on. You know you need a break," said Sunny, the chocolate-faced girl who had been so sweet to her since her first day. "I'll drive you home afterward."

"Just a couple of drinks," Mel encouraged.

Savannah sighed. She hadn't taken in any nightlife since arriving in London. And she wasn't in any hurry to get home to Nyle.

"Okay," said Savannah. "I'll go. But just for a little while."

"Great!"

She dialed her home phone. Called Nyle to let her know that she would be late. "I'm going out with the girls for a little while," she told her.

"Where?"

"What's the name of the place?" She held her hand over the receiver and asked Sunny.

"We'll probably hit a couple," Mel interjected, "but we'll start with Dirty Martini for happy hour."

"So we're club-hopping?" Savannah asked. "I thought we were going for a couple of drinks somewhere."

"We're going to Dirty Martini. St. Paul's location," Sunny said as she shushed Mel. "You'll scare the poor girl off."

"We're going to a place called Dirty Martini," Savannah told Nyle. "St. Paul's location."

"I've heard of it. Have a good time, and be careful," said Nyle. "I'll put you a plate up."

"Thanks," she said.

Savannah noted that Nyle almost sounded motherly. A light smile danced in the corner of her mouth as she grabbed her purse and joined Mel and Sunny at the huge silver elevators.

"This is going to be so much fun!" Mel exclaimed. "Lots of cute guys!"

"Savannah's not interested in cute guys," Sunny said. "She has a guy."

"Ex-guy," Mel corrected her.

"She still loves him," said Sunny. "Isn't that right, Savannah?"

They had been discussing her life as if she weren't standing there.

"We're still close friends. Co-parents to our daughter, if you will."

"Seems like a bit more than co-parenting, darling. You're messaging with him too many hours in the day."

"So he's a friend with benefits, eh, Savannah?" Mel asked.

"Just friends, no benefits."

"If you say so, darling." Mel hooked her arm inside of Savannah's as they walked toward Sunny's compact car. Mel hopped in and stretched her legs across the backseat. Savannah got in on the passenger's side and fastened her seat belt. Sunny blasted her stereo.

The music bounced against the brick walls, and bright lights spanned the room. They managed to snag a corner booth and each of them slid into it. They laughed and talked over the music.

"First round of drinks on me," Sunny said. "What are you having, Savannah?"

"Maybe a glass of wine," said Savannah.

"Are you kidding me?" Mel asked. "No way! You can't come to a place called Dirty Martini and not get a dirty martini!"

"I don't want a martini." Sunny missed her protest, because she'd already headed to the bar.

When she returned, Sunny placed the cocktail in front of Savannah. "Drink up," she said.

"Unwind," Mel said as she sipped on a vodka tonic. "And cheer up. You look like you've lost your best friend."

A tall, handsome man approached the table, whispered something into Sunny's ear. He grabbed her by the hand and pulled her onto the dance floor.

"Well, he was yummy." Mel gave Savannah a wide grin. She held her glass in the air. "Cheers, my friend."

Savannah lifted her glass and toasted with Mel. "Cheers."

"What are we cheering?" asked a blond-haired gentleman as he approached the table. "Is it someone's birthday?"

"We're cheering my friend's arrival to London."

"You're new here?" he asked.

"Yes," Savannah shouted over the music.

"Welcome!" he said, and held his hand out to her. "I'm Louis."

"Hello, Louis. I'm Savannah, and this is Mel."

Louis and Mel shook hands.

"Would you care to dance, Savannah?"

"No, thank you." Savannah gave him a smile. "But my friend Mel here is dying to dance."

"Well, we can't have her dying, now can we?" he asked, and held his hand out to Mel.

Mel gave Savannah a squint of the eyes and a tightened fist behind Louis's back as she followed him to the dance floor. They disappeared into the crowd and Savannah eased her legs onto the leather seat. She sipped on her drink and sat with her back against the wall. She hoped that it wouldn't be a long night, but she was already ready to go. She pulled her cell phone out of her purse and logged in to Facebook. She hadn't heard from Edward in two days. They'd argued about something frivolous and had ended their conversation on a bad note. And he hadn't responded to her message from the night before. She missed him, and hoped he would get past it.

When Sunny returned, Savannah slid out of the booth.

"I need to go to the little girls' room," she said.

"Do you need me to go with you?" Sunny asked.

"I think I'll be fine." Savannah made her way through the crowded nightclub.

She found the restrooms, but there was a long line to get in. So she snagged a place behind a girl who was yapping on her cell phone. The line slowly inched along, and Savannah became impatient. What was she doing here, at this club, in this line, in this country? Why wasn't she at home—her real home—in her warm bed, reading a bedtime story to her child? She'd even rather be arguing with Edward over Chloe's hair, or what extracurricular activities she should participate in. Nyle was right—she was homesick.

"Are you here alone?" someone whispered in her ear.

"No, I'm not," she said sternly without even looking around.

"Are you here with your man?" whispered the intruder.

"No."

"Well, can I be your man?" The voice then sounded familiar.

She turned to face her intruder and found Edward's beautiful eyes looking back at her. He wore blue jeans and a gray cashmere sweater. He had a fresh haircut. She loved when his hair was freshly cut. It made him look so handsome. Her mouth dropped open at the sight of him. And then she cried. Tears crept down the side of her face.

"Not happy to see me?"

She wrapped her arms tightly around his neck, buried her face in his chest. "What are you doing here?"

He didn't respond. Instead he hungrily kissed her lips. "You want me to leave?" he asked.

"No," she whispered, and tears continued to fill her eyes. Whatever they'd argued about two days ago had quickly dissipated. She didn't care about anything or anyone else before this moment. "I'm so glad you're here."

She didn't want to let him go.

"Are you still in line?" asked the woman behind her.

She motioned for the woman to go ahead of her.

"What are you doing here? When did you get here? How did you find me? Where's Chloe?" She asked Edward a million questions.

"She's with your mother," he said.

"You left her with Nyle?"

"She seemed harmless," said Edward.

"We have to go," Savannah said, and grabbed Edward's hand. She led him through the crowd and back to the table where Mel and Sunny sat.

"Well, he's a cutie," Mel said. "You find him in the toilet?"

"This is Edward," Savannah said. "Edward, this is Mel and Sunny. We work together."

"Pleased to meet you both," Edward said.

"No wonder she's still in love with you. You're drop-dead gorgeous!" Sunny said.

"Scrumptious." Mel smiled, licked her lips and gave him a wink.

"We're gonna go," said Savannah, and then she turned to Edward. "How did you get here?"

"Some dude named Xander. He's a friend of your mother's." Edward pointed toward the door. "He's waiting outside."

"Not Xander," mumbled Savannah.

"Who is he?"

"I'll explain later," she said. "Ladies, thanks for inviting me out. It was fun. And I'll see you both on Monday."

"Will you?" Mel asked with raised eyebrows.

"I don't know," she said. Honestly, she didn't know how much more of the job or London she could take.

"Do you have a brother or cousin, or someone who bears a strong resemblance to you?" Mel asked Edward.

"Let's go." Savannah slid her hand into his.

She felt more content and happier than she had in weeks.

Chapter 25

Edward tried to hand Xander a twenty-dollar bill, but he turned it down. Savannah gave Xander a look of skepticism, and Edward wondered what had happened to make her treat him so rudely. He stepped out of the cab and then reached for her. He placed his hand gently around her waist. He wasn't sure how she would react to his showing up unannounced, but he was grateful for the welcome that he received. He'd taken a chance, scrambling for Chloe a passport at the last minute and purchasing two expensive airline tickets. And even as he and Chloe had boarded the flight, he still felt uneasy.

He had tightened Chloe's seat belt around her waist and then secured his. He listened as the flight attendant gave instructions on what to do—and what not to do—in case of emergency. He glanced out the window. It was starting to rain, and he wasn't looking forward to the long flight. But he was looking forward to seeing Savannah. It had only been a few weeks since she left, but it felt like a few months.

He knew that he was taking a chance by coming, but he

needed to fight for her. Finally. If that meant that he had to fly clear across the world to let her know what he was feeling, then he was willing to do that. He needed to let her know how much she meant to him, and that she was wrong about Quinn. He slid his hand into the pocket of his jeans, pulled the emerald out and gave it a quick glance. He was going to get his woman.

Edward and Chloe had slid into the backseat of a hackney cab and he'd given the driver the address that Savannah had given him in case of emergency. She and her mother had been ejected from one place, and she was renting a flat somewhere. The cab pulled up in front of the white brick place, and Edward stepped out and lifted his bags out of the trunk.

"Thank you," he told the driver and gave him a hefty tip and a strong handshake.

He and Chloe stood at the door and rang the bell. When the door swung open, he was surprised to see the beautiful woman who stood on the other side. She was an older yet beautiful replica of Savannah. Her skin was more ivory-colored, but her features were very much like his ex-wife's. He couldn't stop staring.

"Hi, I'm..."

"Edward!" she said before he could finish his sentence.

"Yes."

"Come inside." She gave him a hug and kept smiling. "I'm Nyle."

"I figured," said Edward.

"And you're Chloe!" Nyle gave her a wide grin.

"Hello," Chloe said, and held on to her father's waist.

"Oh my! Did Savannah know that you two were coming?"

"No," Edward said. "We're here to surprise her."

"Boy, she'll be so surprised. And so happy to see you. I think she's quite miserable here."

"She is?" Edward asked.

"She's a good sport. She wanted to make this thing work, she really did. But she's terribly homesick. She needs you two more than she needs me."

"Where is she?"

"She went out for drinks after work."

"She has a job?"

"Yes. Something temporary, just until she lands something permanent."

Edward and Chloe stood in the middle of the floor.

"Sit down. Take a load off," said Nyle. She grinned at Edward. "You're way more gorgeous than I imagined."

"So are you," Edward said.

"Well, aren't you a sweet one. No wonder my daughter's in love with you."

"She's in love with me?" he asked. "Did she tell you that?"

"She didn't have to. Anyone could see," Nyle said. "Do you love her?"

Edward felt uneasy discussing such an intimate subject with someone he hadn't known for more than five minutes. But he couldn't bring himself to lie. "I do love her."

She squealed. "Yes! I knew it. If she loves you, and you love her, then what's the problem?"

Edward unbuttoned the top button of his cardigan. "There's no problem."

"Well, you don't have to talk to me about it." Nyle smiled. "Why don't you go tell her? She's at a place called Dirty Martini. It's a club where the youngsters hang out. Not far from here, and I have a friend who can drive you there."

It hadn't taken much convincing before Edward was in the backseat of a cab and headed to get his woman. There was some reluctance to leave Chloe with Nyle, but he didn't have a choice. He hoped that Savannah wouldn't be too upset about his rash decision. But he was prepared for anything, even if she turned him away.

Now as they stepped into her flat, the aroma of onions and garlic filled the home. Nyle stood at the stove stirring a pot of something, and Chloe stood on a step stool beside her. Savannah obviously hadn't picked up her mother's cooking skills, Edward thought. But he hoped that Chloe would. She tossed vegetables into the pot that Nyle stirred. They were both singing the lyrics of an Adele song. Edward and Savannah stood in the doorway for a moment and observed the duo. When Chloe finally spotted her mother, she hopped from the stool and into Savannah's arms.

"Mommy!"

"Oh, little girl, I've missed you!" Savannah showered her face with kisses. "What are you doing?"

"Me and Gigi are making lamb soup!"

"You and Gigi?" Savannah glanced at Nyle.

"Sounds much more glamorous than Grandmum."

"What else have you and Gigi done today?" Savannah asked.

"We danced." Chloe waved her hands in the air.

"I see," said Savannah. "I've missed you so much!"

"Missed you, too, Mommy."

"Now this is the first smile that I've seen in weeks. You two have made her happy again." Nyle smiled gently. "Why don't you two go find something to do? Let Chloe and me finish dinner." She pushed them both out of the kitchen. "Go. Go have some fun."

* * *

Edward and Savannah did just that. They started with a walk to the Tube and hopped onto it.

"Where are we going?" Edward asked.

"I don't know. Anywhere!" She smiled.

They took the Tube to one of London's rooftop bars. They sipped martinis at the legendary Dukes Hotel bar, and then took the Tube to one of London's oldest wine bars and snagged a table in the dark cave-like bar. A candle burned in the center of the table. They grabbed a wine list and ordered a bottle of Riesling, with a cheese plate to share. Edward couldn't help gazing at the beautiful woman who sat across from him at the table. His eyes wouldn't leave her.

"You're staring," she reminded him.

"I can't help it." Edward reached into his pocket and pulled the engagement ring out. He needed to do this sooner than later, couldn't afford any more missed opportunities. "I love you, Savannah. I never stopped loving you. My heart was ripped apart when you left, but I didn't have the guts to tell you that I couldn't live without you."

Savannah covered her mouth as she hung on every word.

"I don't care about Quinn. I never have, and if she makes you uncomfortable, she's history. I just want my family back." He looked her deeply in her eyes. "Savannah Carrington, will you marry me? Again?" he asked.

The ringing of her phone interrupted their moment. Savannah looked at the screen. "I have to get it. It's Nyle."

"Give me an answer first."

She held her finger in the air and answered the call. "Hello."

"Savannah, it's me. Chloe's running a really high fever,

a hundred and five, and I think I should take her to the emergency room. She doesn't look good."

"Yes, yes, you should take her. Where's the nearest hospital?"

"Chelsea and Westminster."

"We'll meet you there," said Savannah. She hung up. "Chloe's running a fever of a hundred and five. We have to go!"

Edward took care of the check and the two rushed outside and hopped into a cab.

Chapter 26

When they arrived at the hospital, Aunt Frances greeted them in the waiting room.

"Aunt Frances!" Savannah exclaimed. When she didn't see Nyle, she suspected that her mother had ditched Chloe and disappeared again. It was her style. "What are you doing here?"

"Nyle called me. She was frantic," said Aunt Frances.

"She pawned Chloe off on you?"

"No, dear. She's in there with her right now. She hasn't left her side." Aunt Frances pointed. "Down the hall on the right."

Savannah didn't wait for the room number. She quickly trotted down the long hallway with shiny buffed floors. Edward struggled to keep up. She peeked into every room until she found her daughter's. Chloe was sound asleep, but Nyle was next to her bed. She stood when they walked in.

"The doctors managed to get her fever down. Her bronchitis has progressed into pneumonia. They're going to keep her."

"Oh my God! Her bronchitis was cleared up weeks ago." She turned to Edward. "Did she get sick again?"

"I wanted to tell you, but I didn't want you to worry." Edward gave her a sheepish look.

"How could you not tell me?" She stormed toward the door, "I need to see the doctor."

"He's gone for the night, honey. He'll be back in the morning," said Nyle. "But you can speak with her nurse."

Edward covered his face. "I shouldn't have brought her here. She wasn't well enough to travel. This is my fault."

"I shouldn't have left her," Savannah said. "What mother leaves her child?"

"Both of you can stop," said Nyle. "It's nobody's fault. You both just need to focus on getting little Chloe well."

Edward wrapped his arm around Savannah, pulled her close. "I'm going for a cup of coffee. Can I bring either of you something back?"

"No, thank you," they said in unison.

After spending a few days at the hospital, Chloe's condition seemed to worsen. Both Nyle and Savannah refused to leave her side. It was there that the mother-daughter duo began their hard conversations, as Savannah described to her mother how she'd let her down.

"Each time you left, you took a piece of me with you."

"I'm sorry."

"I hated you. I didn't respect you. I pretended you were dead."

"I deserved that." Nyle sat up in the uncomfortable chair that she'd been sleeping in for days. She stretched her legs.

"But then something clicked when I got older. I felt like I was incomplete without it. Felt like I needed to come here and…complete myself. Like somehow, you would make me a whole person," said Savannah. "When all along, I was already complete. I already had everything that I needed."

"I'm glad you came anyway," Nyle said.

"So that you could humiliate me by getting me thrown out onto the street in the middle of the night?" Savannah spat. "You're too old for your shenanigans."

"You're absolutely right."

Nyle apologized to Savannah for not being a good mother, or a mother at all, for that matter. And she promised that her behavior would change. Chloe had somehow touched her heart, and she wanted to be a better example for her granddaughter.

"Something happened to me when little Chloe walked into that door the other day," said Nyle. "I hope that you will allow me to love her."

"What about loving me?" Savannah stood in a huff. She stormed out of the room.

She needed to breathe. She had just unleashed a lifetime of emotions and thoughts onto Nyle in a matter of days. Suddenly she felt a sense of release. Exhaled. How dare her—wanting to love Chloe! She didn't deserve the privilege, and Savannah wouldn't allow it. She would deny *her* this time. She'd been on the receiving end of Nyle's grief; now it was her turn. Make her feel what she'd endured her whole life—wanting to love someone, but not being allowed to do so.

Within a few days, Chloe's condition had progressed a bit and she was out of the woods. Finally, the doctor thought she was getting better, and she would be released from the hospital with a prescription for antibiotics and an order for plenty of fluids and rest. Nyle wanted to stay with her on her last night.

"Why don't you leave her with me for the night. She's doing much better, and you two could use a break," Nyle told Savannah and Edward. "Go enjoy this romantic city. There's nothing wrong with finding love a second time."

Savannah was hesitant at first. She'd already told herself that she wouldn't allow Nyle to spend any quality time with Chloe. But the truth was, she needed a good night's rest—something other than being cramped in a leather chair in the corner of a hospital room. And she needed to be alone with Edward—badly.

"If anything goes wrong, anything at all, you call me," Savannah warned. "If she coughs funny, I wanna know about it."

"I promise."

"Okay." Savannah gave Nyle a half smile. "We're leaving."

She kissed Chloe on the forehead and explained that she would be there first thing in the morning to take her home.

"Are you okay if Mommy leaves?" she asked.

"Is Gigi staying?"

"Yes. She's going to stay with you."

"Okay." Chloe almost smiled. She was comfortable staying with Gigi. The two had become old chums by the end of the week.

"Try to get some rest," said Savannah. "I love you."

"Love you, too, Mommy."

Edward tapped his cheek for Chloe to kiss him. She did. "See you in the morning, sweetheart," he told her.

He managed to pry Savannah away from the room and get her into a cab.

At Savannah's rented flat, they sipped on some aged wine, a bottle that Savannah had saved for a special occasion. Savannah spread a blanket on the living room floor while Edward placed wood in the fireplace. He lay on the floor and beckoned for Savannah to join him.

"Come here, love."

She collapsed onto the floor and found safety in his arms. His lips met hers and he lifted her shirt, placed his cold hand against her skin. He squeezed her right breast. He pulled her shirt over her head and then unhooked her bra. He slowly unbuttoned her jeans and pulled them off, slipped his fingers beneath the elastic of her panties and sank them deep into her sweetness. She moaned.

He buried his face in the crease of her neck and gently kissed her shoulder. He left a trail of kisses between her breasts before taking one between his lips. He licked her nipple and then kissed the other one with the same tenderness. He nibbled on her navel and planted kisses between her thighs. When she felt his tongue dancing, she curled her toes. He savored the taste of her and drove her crazy. He moved his lips back up to hers and kissed her tenderly. He eased himself inside her and made love to her on the floor in front of the fireplace.

She hadn't given Edward an answer to his marriage proposal. She had been too afraid. Afraid that they were rushing into things, that their lives would be too complicated or that they would fail at marriage again.

"I want you to come home," Edward whispered. "We can make this work."

"What makes you so sure? It didn't work the first time."

"I was young and stupid. But now I get it. Now I'm ready to make the sacrifices," said Edward. "I never stopped loving you, Savannah. But I didn't realize it until we were in the Bahamas."

"What about Quinn?"

"She told me what she did. She answered my phone and lied about what was going on. Nothing ever happened between us, Savannah. Not ever. You have to believe me," he said.

She searched his eyes, as if looking for the truth. "I believe you."

He exhaled. He needed to hear those words.

"What about the campaign?" she asked.

"I don't want to run for office. Not if it means compromising my family. You and Chloe are my family. And baby, I choose you."

"Really?"

"Yes, really," said Edward.

"I choose you, too," she said.

He vowed to give her whatever she wanted just to have her in his life. He kissed her lips. "I'll take care of you. Protect you."

"You promise?"

"I promise."

"Then, yes. I will marry you again."

The ramifications of their love, they would consider later. But for now, he had her, and she had him.

Chapter 27

Chloe had finally left the hospital, and Savannah had already made the decision to return to Florida. There were a few loose ends she needed to tie up before leaving London. She needed to visit the doctor's office where she worked, turn in her notice of employment termination and say goodbye to her friends—the ones Edward had met at the club that night. She also needed to meet with the fellow whom she'd rented the flat from, to end their rental arrangement.

As soon as Savannah left to tend to her errands, Edward, Nyle and Chloe had prepared a traditional English meal, and finished it. By midafternoon, Nyle had given Edward a hard lesson in the game of bridge. He was the king of spades and knew bid whist like the back of his hand, but bridge was a game he had never played. As he sat there, he knew that he hadn't quite mastered the game. Chloe, with a baseball cap turned backward on her head, kept score.

The music was loud as a British rap artist spewed his lyrics, and Nyle sipped on a Bloody Mary. She laughed long and hard when Edward lost yet another hand.

"Okay, off with the pants!" she said.

"I'm not taking my pants off, Nyle. This isn't strip bridge." Edward sipped his Bloody Mary. "I'll take off a sock."

"A sock?" Nyle pouted. "That's it?"

"That's it."

"What do you think, madam?" she asked Chloe.

"A sock is fine." Chloe covered her mouth and giggled. She sipped apple juice through a straw.

"Okay, fine," said Nyle. "Off with it."

Edward removed his trouser sock, slapped it onto the table. "There!"

By four o'clock, the trio had become old friends. The music was so loud and they were so engaged in the game of bridge, they didn't even hear Savannah walk through the door.

"Edward?" she asked.

Edward stood, barefoot and shirtless.

"Mommy!" Chloe yelled and rushed into Savannah's arms.

"Hi, baby. Looks like you're feeling better," said Savannah. "Edward, what's going on?"

"We were just playing a game of bridge."

"Nyle, you've been smoking in the house," Savannah said.

Nyle gave her a sheepish grin. "I'm sorry, darling."

Savannah sighed. "I quit my job today, and I called Rolf and told him that I'd be moving out of the flat. What will you do?"

"Oh, don't worry about me. I'll go soften up Aunt Frances. That old woman won't let me sleep on the street."

"I'm going to pack my things."

Edward put his shirt back on, buttoned it and followed Savannah to her bedroom, tapped on the door. He pulled the door open. She sat on the edge of the bed. When he walked in and shut the door behind him, she stood and busied herself around the room.

"Savannah. I know when you walked in…it looked like…"

"Like you and Nyle were having a pretty good afternoon, and you were half naked in my living room."

"I like her. She's cool." Edward laughed, but then dropped his smile when he saw that Savannah was not amused.

Tears burned Savannah's eyes. "It was a mistake coming here."

Edward grabbed her and held on to her. Kissed her tears away. "I don't think it was a mistake. I think it was necessary for you to come here, spend some time with her."

She looked at him with surprise. "I don't know."

"None of us is perfect, Savannah. She was a lousy mother, but she's an okay person. And she loves you. Loves Chloe, too."

"I know."

"Don't judge her too harshly." He pulled her close to him. Wrapped his arms tightly around her. His lips found hers. His tongue danced against hers. He grabbed her face in his hands and looked into her brown eyes. "She's a trip, though. You know that, right?"

"You don't know the half of it," said Savannah. "She's a piece of work."

"Yes."

"She damn near charmed you out of your drawers."

"She didn't charm me out of my drawers."

"Almost."

Edward kissed her lips again. He was glad to have her

back in his arms and his life. And soon they would share the same home again. He knew that, with love, they could handle most anything.

Chapter 28

Leaving London was bittersweet for Savannah. She and her mother hadn't bonded as she'd hoped, and she wasn't sure that they ever would. But Nyle and Chloe *had* connected. It was the first time her mother had displayed anything maternal, and she almost hated to separate the two of them.

"I'll come visit," Nyle told Chloe.

"You promise?" asked Chloe as she held on to her Gigi.

"I promise, little one. Don't you worry."

It was the same promise that Savannah had heard from Nyle her entire life. Chloe would be just as disappointed as she'd been as a child. Waiting for Nyle to return, but she never would.

"If you happen to be in the States, look us up." Savannah gave her mother a quick hug and broke away just as quickly. Tears filled her eyes, but she hid them. She knew that this would be the last time she'd pursue her mother again. She had finally accepted that Nyle Carrington would never change, and that she would never be the mother she needed in her life. She had come to terms with that.

"I'll do that," said Nyle.

Edward lifted their bags out of the trunk and set them at the curb. He glanced at their airline tickets and then at his watch. "We should get going if we're going to make our flight."

Nyle hugged Savannah, then Edward. She gave Chloe a strong hug and then lit an herbal cigarette. She hopped into the front seat of Xander's cab and let the window down, rested her chin on the door.

As he pulled away from the curb, she yelled out the window. "Go make me some more grandchildren. I need about five more like her!"

"Bye, Gigi!" Chloe yelled.

"Bye, my little Chloe. Be sweet!" she hollered back.

"I will."

Savannah watched as the hackney carriage disappeared into traffic. She shook her head, and a slight smile danced in the corner of her mouth. She sighed and followed Edward through the airport's automatic doors.

The plane ride home didn't seem as long as it had coming. She and Edward laughed and discussed the antics of Nyle. Savannah wondered how she would survive without someone there to keep her in line. She hoped that she would manage to get her life together. They talked about their future together and what it would look like.

"I don't want another wedding. Do you?" asked Savannah.

"I want what you want."

"I think we can just go to the justice of the peace," she said.

"I don't care about the formalities, I just want you." Edward grabbed her hand and held on to it.

"Maybe we can have a barbecue or some little get-together. Invite our friends."

"Okay."

"I need to call my daddy," said Savannah. "Let him know."

"He won't be happy for us. He still blames me for hurting you the first time."

"He just wants what's best for me. And once he sees how happy I am, he'll be happy for us."

Edward looked at her. "I should call him. Tell him myself. I called him the first time…asked him for your hand in marriage. I'll call him again."

"You sure?"

"No. But I'm a man. I can do this."

Savannah placed her hand gently against his cheek. "You are a man. My man."

Edward leaned over and kissed her lips. "I can't wait to call my parents. They'll be thrilled. They love you."

"And I love them." Savannah smiled.

"We should plan another trip there. Soon."

"I'm always up for a trip to the Bahamas," she said.

They discussed their finances and taking the house off the market. They would remain in their dream home—the one they'd built together the first time around. It was a perfectly good house. Edward would sell his house instead.

Savannah was thrilled to see the Florida palm trees that she'd missed so much. She inhaled the moist air and breathed in the smell of the ocean. It was great to be home. Edward took the scenic route and then pulled the car into the driveway of their home. She appreciated the thought of *their* home. They would soon be a family again, and living under one roof. He would be her man again, her husband, her lover. She looked at the emerald on her finger and smiled.

"Take Chloe in and get her settled. I'll get the bags," he said and stepped out of the car.

Savannah helped her daughter out of her seat and led her into the house. She started her a warm bath and found a pair of pajamas. She tucked Chloe into bed and turned off the light. She rushed to her bedroom and ran her own bath, squeezed bubbles into the tub. She laid out her favorite pair of lace panties—a pair she'd picked up at Victoria's Secret months ago, but had never worn. She didn't even know why she bothered. But tonight she was glad she had. It would be her first night with Edward in their home.

She lit a few candles and then turned down the lights. She stepped into the tub and relaxed against the porcelain, closed her eyes and listened as Marvin Gaye's "Let's Get It On" filled the master bathroom. When she heard the light tap on the door, she opened her eyes as Edward walked in.

"Care if I join you?" he asked.

"Not at all," she said. "Where have you been?"

"Caught the end of the game. Thought I'd come and see what you were up to."

He shut the door, and when he returned he was completely naked. Savannah admired the beauty of his chiseled, well-endowed body. She'd missed it. Those strong arms had always held her close, kept her safe. Those legs had braced her when she'd found herself on top. She'd rested her head on that chest more times than she could count. And what lay between his thighs had given her so much pleasure.

He stepped into the bathtub and took a seat behind her. He wrapped his arms tightly around her and caressed her breasts, pinched her tender nipples. He squeezed shower gel into his palms, lathered it, and caressed her. This time he gently planted kisses against the back of her neck. She moaned when his fingertips found their way between her legs, danced there until she couldn't stand it any longer.

"Welcome home," she whispered.

"It's so good to be home," he said.

She relaxed her head against his chest, and he wrapped his arms tightly around her. He held her until Marvin finished singing about sexual healing. She turned around in the tub and washed his chest, arms and parts that belonged to her again. She kissed his lips and rested her behind on his hardness until she felt him inside her, wrapped her legs around his waist. He grabbed the roundness of her cheeks and squeezed.

She loved him again. In fact, she'd never stopped. And all things were well again in the Talbot household.

Chapter 29

The first thing Edward wanted to do was take Savannah and Chloe to his parents' home on Eleuthera, Bahamas. Show them off. Let everyone know that they'd been right all along—he *did* still love Savannah, and they were a family again. When they heard the news of the engagement, they insisted on a celebration in the couple's honor at the Grove. It was a happy time for the Talbot family.

Savannah wore a navy blue after-five dress with a one-shoulder silhouette. Edward wore a navy tie that accented his gray suit. The Grove was beautifully decorated in navy and silver, and crystal lights beamed throughout the Grand Room. White roses were sprinkled about, and silver candles burned on every table. A traditional Caribbean meal was prepared—baked cod, conch fritters, conch salad and Edward's favorite papaya soup. Raquel had captured his recipe down to the smallest ingredient.

Music filled the Grand Room, and Edward stood next to his two favorite girls. He beamed with pride and his heart was filled with joy. His life would be different—his family had become his priority, and his career had taken a backseat.

He was a new man. All the Talbots were in attendance. Even Denny had flown in early that morning. He held on to Sage's hand. Edward was happy to see that his younger brother had manned up and patched things up with his ex-fiancée. He knew that a good woman was a rare commodity, and losing one was unacceptable. Edward could attest to this, and he didn't want to see his brother endure the same pain.

When Edward saw Nate, he went over to him.

"Little brother." He reached for Nate's hand.

Nate embraced him. "I'm sorry."

"Water under the bridge," said Edward. "You only spoke the truth."

"I'm glad you got your girl," Nate said. "Happy that you found love again."

"What about you? Will you find love again?" asked Edward.

"Probably not. But I'm okay with that. I'm happy to be alone."

"No one should be alone. It's a lonely world out there," said Edward. "Maybe you'll find a woman…*or not*…someday."

Edward was in denial about his brother's sexuality. He'd chosen not to think about it.

"Maybe."

Jasmine's voice interrupted their moment. She grabbed the microphone and tapped on it to see if it was on.

"Hello."

"I think it's on," Edward told her.

"I'd like to make an announcement," she began. "Where's Jackson?"

Jackson raised his hand in the air as if he were in an elementary school classroom.

"Come up here, babe."

Jackson maneuvered his way through the crowd and stood next to Jasmine.

"We would like to announce that we are with child..."

Jackson looked shocked. It was the first he'd heard of it. "We are?" he asked.

She grabbed his hands in hers and placed them on her stomach. "I don't mean to steal your moment, Edward and Savannah."

"It's okay," said Edward. "Congratulations."

Jackson grabbed Jasmine in his arms, lifted her in the air. He beamed with pride as Jasmine grabbed his face in her hands. She kissed his lips. Edward remembered what that moment felt like—the moment when he first learned that Chloe was growing inside Savannah's stomach. He had rushed out and purchased a soccer ball and a baseball glove, had the glove engraved with the Talbot name. He had plans of teaching his son the basics of soccer. He would encourage him to follow his footsteps in politics. He felt a bit of disappointment when the doctor announced that his son was a daughter instead. He even walked out of the room to gather himself. When he returned and held that little girl in his arms, he felt better. But the first time she peered into his eyes and gave him a half smile, his heart melted. Chloe had him doing her every bidding since that moment.

"Just hope it's not a girl," Edward whispered to Jackson. "You're doomed if it is. She'll have you wrapped around her skinny little finger before you know what's going on."

"I'm confident that it's not a girl," said Jackson. "I don't make girls."

Edward's laughter caught the attention of his sister.

"What are you two over here laughing about?" Jasmine asked.

"Nothing," the two of them said in unison.

Edward finally retrieved the microphone from his sister. He offered a toast to his bride-to-be. He talked about how lucky he was to have her back in his life, and he meant every word of it. He looked at his parents. His father held on tightly to his mother's waist. Their love was a true example of what it was supposed to look like. If he could keep Savannah contented for that many years, he would die a happy man. He held his glass in the air, and so did everyone in the room.

"Cheers!" he said.

"Cheers!" the crowd repeated.

He kissed Savannah's lips, and everyone applauded.

After the toast, Edward glanced across the room and spotted a familiar face in the midst of the crowd. Nyle raised a champagne flute into the air, a wide grin on her face. He gave her a wink. Savannah spotted her, too, and he watched as she sighed deeply. He had to admit it was good seeing Nyle, and he knew that Savannah would feel the same way. Although things hadn't worked out for her in London, he knew that she still loved her mother and had hopes of salvaging some type of relationship with her. Perhaps there was hope for them after all.

Everything in Savannah's life seemed to be falling right into place. She'd even been successful at finding work with another fashion design company in Florida, and Edward was happy about that. He'd assured her that she didn't need to work, that he would take care of them. But Savannah loved her career, and fashion had been her lifeline. She wanted to work.

Chloe had already reconnected with her Gigi and the two were engaged in a conversation. At that moment, he knew that whatever Nyle had missed with Savannah, she would regain through Chloe. The two had become friends. He knew they would. And he knew that she had been excited about his and Savannah's newfound love, which was why he'd sent her an airline ticket to the Bahamas. He wanted her there to share their moment.

"She's coming to stay in Florida with us for a little while," he whispered to Savannah. "Is that okay?"

She gave him a genuine smile and a nod. A tear crept down the side of her face.

"I love you," she whispered in his ear.

"I love you more."

Edward gazed in her eyes and made a note of how happy she looked at that moment. Her heart was full, and so was his. He'd managed to snag the woman of his dreams and sweep her off of her feet—*again*. Which only proved that love really was sweeter the second time around.

* * * * *